MW01125578

THE EARTHFLEET SAGA

Volume Two

By

Dennis Young

© All story material Dennis Young 2019

No part of this book may be used or reproduced by any means, graphic, electronic, or mechanical, including photocopying, recording, taping, or by any information storage retrieval system without the written permission of the author(s), except in the case of brief quotations embodied in critical articles and reviews.

This is a work of fiction. All characters, names, incidents, organizations, and dialogue in this book are either the products of the author's imagination or used fictitiously. Any resemblance to actual persons, living or dead, or actual events is purely coincidental.

Because of the dynamic nature of the Internet, any web addresses or links contained in this book may have changed since publication and may no longer be valid. The views expressed in this work are solely those of the author(s).

ISBN-13:9781796996111

Printed in the United States of America.
First published March 2019

THE EARTHFLEET SAGA

Volume Two

THE EARTHFLEET SAGA TIMELINE

The year is 2554 (Old Calendar). Earth continues its recovery from the most devastating wars ever waged. Half the planet is uninhabitable. The other half is overrun with refugees, those ill from effects of fission and fusion weapon use, and diseases that followed. The human population has been reduced by nearly sixty percent. Radiation levels worldwide range from dangerous to lethal.

Infertility and birth mutations have increased infant mortality to thirty-eight percent. Crop growth has been cut in half. Sea life has suffered at a reduced, but undetermined, rate. Beaches all over the world have been littered with dead sea life for nearly a hundred years. Land fauna and flora have suffered drastic losses.

Somehow, in the western North American continent, in what was once called disparagingly the "Left Coast", a pocket of survivors is building a new future. Having commandeered the three remaining space stations orbiting Earth, the main Lunar military establishment, and partnered with the two friendly Martian colony strongholds, Earth Alliance arises. With the best and brightest, in the space of only fifty years following the war, they began to deal with the devastation and desolation that was left.

The job is far from finished. In fact, it is only now beginning. Earth, the Cradle of Mankind, is all but done. And with the resources of the Moon, Mars, and the Allied Asteroid Belt States, Earth Alliance is now looking beyond Earth. Beyond the Solar System. Beyond that very desolation and destruction.

Earth Alliance is looking to the Stars.

In the late 2300's, the Millennium Project and the Outward Presence Movement began. Generational ships, needing decades to cross the abyss of Space to the closest habitable planets, moved at less than the speed of light. Some never made their destinations, succumbing to the hazards of Space, or of humans confined too long in a limited, struggling, artificial environment. Yet some succeeded.

In the early 2400's, the greatest breakthrough in spaceflight was made, and the Lightspeed Barrier was breached. Ships built for sublight travel were quickly modified. New ships were designed and built. Launchings occurred once per year, on the day that became known simply as *Naissance.* Problems with artificial gravity, environmental systems, and weapons for defense were branched off from the discoveries made by HyperLight Systems.

But as with every advance in Mankind's history, a price was extracted. Humans were, after all, still humans. And while many colonies flourished, others did not. Some became ill-managed. Others simply decided their best course of action was piracy. Several became openly hostile toward Mother Earth. Because politics, as always, never died. It only hid for a while. Waiting. Watching. Planning.

Earthfleet arose, and grew in size and power. A dream for many decades, it became a force within the Earth Alliance, a loose alliance of planets colonized by humans. Again, politics came into play, but this time, with the strength of Earthfleet behind it. It was a benevolent ruling system for the most part, but with teeth. And to this day, still is.

And as Earthfleet probed the outer reaches of unexplored territory, new races were found; alien races, unlike anything Earth had ever seen. The adage was, "Little Green Men existed, but they were neither little, nor green."

There are five known alien species. Three are xenophobic, adversarial, and, in two cases, openly hostile. Skirmishes have occurred, though to this time, hostilities have been short-lived, if deadly. For nearly a hundred years Earthfleet has dealt with these challenges.

But as with any advancing and expanding culture, confrontations have become more frequent. Disagreements over territories (planets and other resources) have required skillful negotiations in many cases, and the application of the "Big Stick" in others.

Such are the ships of Earthfleet. While exploration of the galaxy is always the First Directive, the vessels are nonetheless more than capable of defending themselves and Earth Alliance interests.

It is an interesting time to be alive... in the *Olde Earth* Chinese sense. And sometimes very, very dangerous.

PORT IN A STORM

Starship Agincourt

By

Dennis Young

Prologue

They were not human, but like humans, they were a curious people. When they found the planet, they first investigated indigenous life and, finding no intelligence above that of lower animals, established a small base.

Once confirmed the planet was habitable, they took time and effort to construct an orbital station, staffed by qualified volunteers who thought it a wondrous experience. After all, the planet was beautiful, with great oceans and tall mountains, obviously in its young maturity; what humans would have called a "Goldilocks" world.

Soon enough, they had amassed data, recorded information, sampled, measured, inspected, and analyzed to the extent they could. Then they departed with their treasures, returning home to the welcomes of their families and friends.

But the station remained, running on auxiliary power, monitoring and continuing to gather anything meaningful or interesting.

Time passed. No one returned. And so, the station followed protocol, shutting down all but the most essential of operations. Life support slowly ceased. Temperatures within the station dropped to barely above the freezing point of water. The station shut down its sensing equipment. The only thing left was the sleep-mode generators, self-initiating meteor-repair systems, motion sensor alarms, and passive scanners.

Until…

One
Battle Stations

"Duty Log, Captain Noah Westermann, 022617.02. EAS Agincourt is in trouble. While investigating a newly-discovered dwarf pulsar, a magnetic storm erupted, damaging our sensor network and hyperlight drive. Numerous casualties were taken, and sickbay is currently operating on auxiliary power to handle the most severe of cases.

If that weren't enough, as the ship headed at flank sublight speed to the singularity border, we were attacked by two Qoearc Tak'nar-class scouts. With our tactical sensors inoperative and targeting computers offline, we took substantial damage before countermeasures could be initiated. Fortunately, we evaded them long enough to get away from the star's gravitational effects and engage hyperlight drive. We're currently running at 120c, the best we can manage, but have no idea if the Qoearc are following, if they've sustained damage as has Agincourt, or exactly what the tactical situation is. Right now, we're flying blind in a general heading only guessed at when we went Over-c. Needless to say, the situation is serious."

* * *

The Command Bridge of EAS Agincourt…

"Tactical, report!" Captain Noah Westermann shot a glance aside to the Science station as his Arneci Tac-Officer swore quietly in her native tongue.

"Nothing, sir, the board is dead. Tech is still chasing gremlins in the system."

Westermann caught her muttering the words *karskat tezha* and nearly laughed, even in their current situation. Arneci were "earthy" he had always known, but Thevoss

Sh'zaoqoq's curses bordered on obscene when she was stressed.

"Belay that, Commander. Just the facts."

"Sorry sir. Sensors are intermittent at best, but no sign of the Qoearc I can detect."

"Sciences?"

Lieutenant Commander Xiaoli's face was impassive as she scanned her readouts. "Confirmed, Captain, we are clear for approximately thirty light-minutes."

"Engineering, status."

"We're draining the tanks, sir. The Chief reports nothing left to give."

Westermann sat back for a moment, then turned to the Comm station. "Report, Lieutenant Skovok."

"No subspace or RF chatter, encrypted or clear, sir." The comm-officer gave a quick nod to Westermann before turning back to his panel.

Westermann blew a breath. "Secure from Battle Stations, go to Standby Alert. Helm, reduce speed to 100c." He punched the intercom button on his command seat arm. "Engineering, Bridge. I need a quick estimate on repairs to the hyperlight drive and environmental systems. Those are the priorities, then weapons. I need your report in fifteen minutes, Commander Ch'virrorh." He clicked off and looked again to Tactical. "Look sharp. Navigation, status."

"Clear ahead, sir, as far as I can tell. Maybe..."

Westermann waited patiently as Lieutenant Butler ran a quick diagnostic.

"Something ahead, but hard to tell exactly... not a ship, though, too large."

"On viewer."

"Viewscreen is down, sir." Butler looked to Tactical.

"Commander Thevoss, can you confirm anything at all?"

Westermann held his comment, waiting.

"Confirmed, Captain, likely a planet, perhaps two light years distant. About seven days travel at current speed."

Westermann hit the intercom again. "Auxiliary Control, Bridge. Lori, get up here as fast as you can. Leave your second in command there." He broke the circuit before receiving an answer. "Keep an eye on things," he said to Butler.

Westermann rose, headed for the lift. "Commander Xiaoli, take the conn until XO Hamilton arrives. I'm going to Sickbay for a bit. Tactical, work with Nav to set a course for the planet and keep a watch for Qoearc or anything else. Get as much information on that planet as you can and set up a conference for the next shift."

A chorus of "aye sir" met his ears just before the lift doors closed.

* * *

Sickbay had calmed from chaos to merely frantic. Dr. Hoshi Kamisori, the Chief Medical Officer, gave a cursory glance to Westermann as he entered, then went back to tending patients. The captain stood aside as medical staff hurried between beds and chairs that had been hastily set around the perimeter of the room for the less-serious cases.

Burns from electrical shortages, broken bones caused when the ship's compensators blipped as the magnetic storm hit, and three serious cases of concussion streamed across the wall charts as Westermann watched. He waited until Kamisori had a moment, then motioned her aside. "Can I get thirty seconds, Doctor? Just give me a summary."

She motioned around. "I have ten cases confined to

their quarters and two nurses attending them. The rest are all right here. What you see is what you get."

"There was no warning of the storm, Doctor. This is no one's fault."

Kamisori gave him a look. "I've heard said we were too close to the pulsar. Is that true?"

Westermann held his words for a long moment. "We were within accepted parameters. Anything else?"

"No." She turned away as Westermann shook his head and took his exit, heading for Engineering.

The corridors were dimly lit, only emergency lighting at low levels to conserve power. Security guards in pairs were stationed at each lift entrance, two of which held the doors open as Westermann approached. He entered and hit the intercom button. "Engineering." The lift moved downward smoothly. Westermann stared blankly at the walls, wondering how this could have happened and why he had made such poor decisions in their doing.

* * *

Lori Hamilton, First Officer of *Agincourt*, stepped onto the Bridge to nods and smiles around. Even Skovok at the Comm station nearly showed a smile, and the mood of the Bridge quickly became less formal.

Hamilton seated herself in the command chair. "Alright ladies and gentlemen, tell me what you've got."

"Tactical is slowly responding, sensors are at ninety percent."

"Engineering has hyperlight capability to 120c, full sublight and thrusters."

"Environmental steady, all systems nominal."

"Sciences confirms the planet, now one-point-eight five

light years distant. Sensors are mostly clear."

Hamilton raised an eyebrow at Xiaoli's comment. "Mostly? Can you be a bit more specific?"

"Eighty percent, Commander. Apologies."

"Don't worry about it, but the captain will insist on accuracy, you know that. Comm?"

"Clear channels, Commander."

Nav, Conn?"

"Helm is answering fully." Nijah Maddani looked over her shoulder. "Good to see you, Commander. We heard it was a bit anxious in AC." She adjusted her hijab and turned back to the controls.

"Nav clear." Butler turned his boyish smile to Hamilton. "I'm working with Commander Sh'zaoqoq to get a better look at the planet."

Hamilton's eyes narrowed. "How old are you, Mister Butler?"

"Twenty-five, Commander."

"And already a full Lieutenant." She grinned. "Hot-shot, are you?"

Butler blushed as Maddani chuckled under her breath. "They call me 'Skip', Commander. I came on board at Fleet Base Twelve about two months ago."

Hamilton nodded. "Carry on, Skip." She straightened in the command chair. "Alright, listen up. We've had a bad situation, but the ship is secure. No one died and no one is to blame. The universe tends toward perverseness, so let's take this as a lesson. We've got a job to do and on top of that, we may have discovered a new planet. So let's see what we have."

The Bridge crew busied themselves as Hamilton took a moment to order tea from the Mess, then sat back, watching the main screens begin to come back to life.

"Commander, I'm picking up ship signatures aft." Xiaoli at Sciences turned to her panel, then back to the scanner. "Three… no, four. Three smaller, one large."

"Distance?"

"They're not following that my instruments can tell. They're still in the vicinity of the star we left and appear to be remaining in the system."

"Confirmed, Commander," said Sh'zaoqoq at Tactical. "Sensors indicate low power levels on all vessels. Three appear to be scouts as the ones that attacked us, the third may be as large as a cruiser." She turned to Hamilton. "Typical Qoearc heavy recon squadron."

"At least as large as a *Cotak* Class," added Xiaoli. "Possibly larger."

Hamilton let go a heavy breath. "So we're at least, what, a day away at max hyperlight?"

"Zero point eight eight standard days at Hyperlight Eight." Xiaoli turned to the command chair. "Accurately."

"Keep an eye on them. If they start to move, let me know immediately. I assume our neutrino trail is still detectable, right?"

"Correct, for at least another standard day."

"They'll be hot on our trail then. My guess is, they took damage like we did, but no telling how long it will take them to get going. Qoearc ships are notoriously light on shielding from storms like the one we encountered."

A steward arrived with tea and Hamilton sipped as she looked around the Bridge. There was little discernable damage other than blank screens and flickering displays. The Bridge crew had stood nearly two full watches, and now that Battle Stations had been cancelled, relief could be provided.

"Comm, alert the second shift. Let's get all of you some food and rest. As soon as your relief arrives, give them updates and stand down until your next duty is scheduled."

The crew breathed a collective sigh of relief.

I know the captain has a lot on his mind, and is probably chastising himself for what happened, but dammit, he's got to start being a bit more aware that this crew isn't a machine… the way he thinks he is.

Relief officers began to arrive in ones and twos. Hamilton watched as updates were given and status of each station posted. She nodded to each of the prime Bridge officers as the filed into the lift, then turned to face the screens again.

"Alright, ladies and gentlemen, let's see what we have…"

* * *

Abol Ch'virrorh straightened as Westermann entered the main engineering complex. Arneci, and bonded mate to Tactical Officer Thevoss Sh'zaoqoq, Ch'virrorh was typical of his Race; somewhat squat in appearance, dark-skinned, nearly hairless, and possessing of eyes having irises and "whites" so dark, they could hardly be discerned from his pupils. Westermann knew those eyes could almost literally see electrical wave patterns, making Ch'virrorh an excellent Chief Engineer; he could see things in the systems that humans could not. Westermann held Ch'virrorh as a real treasure to *Agincourt*; and a good friend.

"Captain, environmental systems are operating at ninety percent nominal. Hyperlight core is stable, but we are running a second diagnostic due to aberrant readings in the first."

Westermann nodded, passing a glance around the engineering deck, noting orderly activity. If nothing else, Ch'virrorh was as thorough in his duties as the captain tried to be in his.

"The Bridge?" Ch'virrorh's question was a quiet and careful one.

"Minimal damage, no injuries." Westermann showed a hint of a smile. "She's fine, Abol. My guess is by now, Commander Hamilton has released the prime Bridge crew and Thevoss is in Sickbay for her routine checkup. Dr. Kamisori will take good care of her."

Ch'virrorh led the captain to his small office space. They sat in quiet for moments as Ch'virrorh mused the words. "I am… sorry to have caused such issue on board, Captain. We did not know of her… condition until we left Fleet Base Twelve."

"Never be sorry for the miracle of life, my friend. Once we return to Base, you can both be reassigned for the duration."

Ch'virrorh looked away. "It is a sentence of the universe, that we should be weak in our ability to carry on our people. Somewhere long ago in our past, someone of the Arnec caused great harm, and now we see… what is the human word… karma?"

Westermann slowly shook his head. "There is no weakness in the Arneci. You face this crisis with dignity and purpose. And any child born of your people is one child more to carry on. Peace, Abol, and strength to you and your bondmates. Earth Alliance will find a way. The Arnec will survive and grow stronger of this."

Ch'virrorh nodded at the last. "Very well. As you say,

stronger. Therefore, we will redouble our repair efforts and have all systems optimal within six hours, Captain."

"Good. In the meantime, turn your orders over to the assistant chief and seek your mate. Take time together until your next duty shift."

"Aye, sir. My gratitude."

They rose and exited the office, Ch'virrorh calling for Lieutenant Marcus, as Westermann headed for the corridor and the lift once more.

* * *

The station sensed them even then. Nearly a light-year away, it knew they were approaching, likely intent upon the planet and unaware of the station's presence yet. Therefore, it kept its recently-awoken sensors trained and only watched. It did not use active sensing. It did not send messages to its place of origin, nor did it prepare defenses. It only waited, intrigued by the unique design of the approaching object. Was it an automaton, or did it have true intelligence of its own? Was it crewed or only machine? Or possibly part of both, as had been found more than once in its creator's investigations. For now, it didn't matter. It knew the vessel approached, and reasoned as it did so, the station would become apparent to whatever processes guided it. Only then would the station decide how best to react.

* * *

Westermann found his way to quarters after checking once again with Sickbay. Dr. Kamisori had been a bit more cordial, confirming only three serious cases after treatments had been completed. She actually smiled as Westermann gave her an official "well done". Or was it only because he was leaving Sickbay again?

With the XO on the Bridge, he could afford a sorely-needed four hours under a sleep-set. He lay down, affixed the head gear, and punched in the timer. In thirty seconds, he was in deep REM sleep.

Four and a half hours later, Westermann sat at his desk with coffee, and drank slowly as he mulled events of the last twenty-four standard hours. The discovery of the dwarf pulsar star, the approach, the flares, the storm. Then the unlikely and far-too-coincidental appearance of the Qoearc. The attack, with *Agincourt* taking damage and casualties; then running for their lives, blinded by the storm, no defenses, no sensors, the Bridge crew holding down their fears like the true professionals they were.

He shook his head and cursed his own poor judgment, then punched the intercom button. "Bridge, Captain. Commander Xiaoli, Commander Sh'zaoqoq, set up a meeting for…" he glanced at the chronometer. "1600 in the main briefing room. All department heads and seconds to attend. I need a full analysis on the events at the star, the attack, ship's condition, and our alternatives at this point. Also, everything you have on this planet we're headed for. Draw whatever resources you need from IT and Intel." He snapped off the switch, leaned back in his chair and blew a heavy breath. He poured another cup and drank again.

Text appeared on his PADD. DO YOU HAVE A FEW MINUTES? XO

Lori. SURE, COME ON DOWN, he typed.

I'M ON THE BRIDGE. THERE IN TEN.

Westermann sighed. *Now I'm gonna get a talkin' to.*

* * *

Hamilton left the Sciences Lieutenant in command as she took leave, headed for Westermann's quarters. All systems were operating nominally, space was clear ahead, and Tactical still showed no sign the Qoearc were pursuing *Agincourt*. And she trusted the Bridge crew, even the second shift. But now, she was due for a break as well, and sorely needed to talk the captain out of his funk. On that, she took her leave, intent on at least a change of uniform before speaking to the captain.

Battle Stations and Qoearc play hell with personal hygiene, she thought as she entered her quarters. *If I stink of burned electronics, maybe he won't notice the sweat.* She smirked as she changed into standard off-duty garb, brushed her hair quickly, and headed out the door.

* * *

"Commander, I'm detecting sensing from the planet." The second shift Tactical Officer ran a quick diagnostic on her Tactical panel, rechecked the readings, and turned to Lieutenant Harman in the command seat.

Harman moved quickly to her Science station and peered into the viewer. "The planet appears to be strong Earth-type. A bit larger than Terra, earlier development, atmosphere in flux… no signs of RF activity."

"Agreed, but still…" Fingers clicked across the Tac Panel. "The board is green. Something on or very close to the planet is watching us. Strictly passive, and the energy output is barely detectable."

"In orbit?" asked the navigator, Ensign Tooley.

"Possible." Harman sharpened the resolution. "Still too far away to tell. Interesting, however. Log the event and include in your points for the briefing. Set an alarm for any change in observational status." She turned to the Tactical board. "And inform the captain, if you please."

* * *

The door chimed as Westermann was pouring his third cup of coffee. "Come in."

Hamilton entered, off-duty fatigues clean and crisp, her long dark hair loose about her shoulders. "Captain."

"Have a seat, Lori. Coffee? Tea? Something stronger?"

"Tea, please." Hamilton took the chair opposite Westermann and waited as he drew from the server. They drank in silence for a few moments.

"You don't ask for a private consultation unless something's wrong. "Westermann blew gently across his cup.

"Concern for the captain. Let's talk about what has happened." Hamilton set down her tea. "A new star, a flare, and the damnedest coincidence of running across the Qoearc I've ever seen."

Westermann considered. "You think they might have followed us?"

"Or were attracted to the star as well. Dwarf pulsars are pretty much an unproven theory, and to run across one is astronomical odds, no pun intended."

Quiet set upon the room for moments. "A trap? Some sort of construct? Lie in wait for unassuming ships? That could be a lot of downtime."

"We found three small ships and a larger one, possibly a cruiser, once sensors were back on line, all still at the star."

Westermann thought again. "Following us?"

Hamilton shook her head. "No, and that sort of blows my theory out of the water. They appear to be more damaged than we were."

"Cheap Qoearc shielding." Westermann grinned at his jest. "What else?"

Hamilton paused before answering. "Captain, you can't beat yourself up for decisions made. Nothing you did was wrong."

"Maybe not wrong, but certainly unwise."

Hamilton drank again. "Sometimes decisions don't take into account the perverseness of the universe. There was no way to predict the flare… or storm… or Qoearc."

"Trouble comes in threes, says the old adage."

"Yes, sir. And so do decisions based on the best available information. Everything you did was by the Book."

Westermann shook his head. "And that's the problem, Lori. I should have seen beyond the Book. I should not have ordered us closer to the star, should not have stayed when the flare hit, and certainly should have anticipated Qoearc. We're less than five light years into unclaimed space. You and I both know how the Qoearc love to provoke engagements."

"Keeps us on our toes, right?" Hamilton smiled and refilled her cup, then drank again. "Let it go, Captain. The ship is secure, the crew is safe, and we're on the way to a previously unknown planet. The silver lining shows through the darkest clouds sometimes."

"Damned optimist." Westermann lifted his cup to her. "Alright, I've been chastised, and I appreciate your concern. Thank you. What else? Odds on more perverseness?"

The intercom buzzed. Westermann raised an eyebrow. Hamilton simply laughed.

* * *

The briefing room filled slowly as department heads

and their seconds entered, taking seats where possible, or standing at the walls around the room. Xiaoli and Sh'zaoqoq stood at the screen which showed a schematic of the system they were approaching, with a target circle around the fifth planet.

Westermann entered and took his chair at the table head, nodded to his science officer. The room quieted.

"This briefing is to update *Agincourt's* status, review events, and discuss options upcoming." Xiaoli's voice was smooth and professional. Westermann nodded to himself, having hand-picked her nearly two years before as a member of his crew.

"As known, the star was discovered during routine patrol in a little-traveled sector. Investigation showed it to be a dwarf pulsar, thought until now to be theoretically impossible. The star is much smaller than Sol but more massive, and has a highly energetic magnetic field."

"Damage to the ship caused by this star?" asked Hamilton as she entered, a moment late.

"Serious to our sensors and environmental systems, Commander. Some issues with hyperlight power that are currently being corrected, and non-life-threatening injuries to twenty-two crew members. Sensors are at ninety percent, EMP shields at sixty-five, and environmental is now stable. Hull damage was negligible from the storm, but the Qoearc attack caused two minor breaches, which have since been repaired."

"What about the Qoearc?" asked Westermann, passing a glance to Hamilton.

Sh'zaoqoq changed the screen to a grainy picture of the pulsar and surrounding area. "Three scouts and one larger ship, all currently dead in space. Our sensors now suggest they have heavy damage to systems and propulsion. Our neutrino wake is dissipating and will be undetectable in six hours. It is doubtful they will be an any shape by then to follow."

"Might they have been tracking us before the... accident?" Skip Butler asked, standing at one side.

Sh'zaoqoq stood straighter. "If so, I deserve a reprimand for not seeing them."

"Belay that, Commander," said Westermann softly. "We don't know they were chasing us, and it could well have been a coincidence. The pulsar might have attracted their attention just like it did ours. No fault in this matter is being considered."

Hamilton gave Westermann a quick smile, then turned her attention back to the screen.

"Commander Xiaoli, what about this planet we're headed for?" Westermann watched the screen change once more, this time to a rather normal-looking blue sphere.

"Earth-like. The atmosphere shows no sign of industrial wastes, no RF signals, and high oxygen content in the air. The two largest continents are covered in vegetation and all mountain ranges appear to be very young."

"New Earth," said the helmswoman Maddani softly. "Beautiful."

"So, uninhabited, correct?" asked Westermann.

"Correct, Captain, as far as intelligence above basic animal life. However, we are detecting scans from the planet's area."

"In orbit," said Sh'zaoqoq, bringing up a new picture on the screen. "A small station, or very large satellite. There are no detectable life signs, very low power indicators, and whatever is watching us is attempting to stay unnoticed. Our tactical sensors register only a taste of indication."

"Taste, Commander?" Skip Butler smiled as he asked the question.

"Touch," Sh'zaoqoq replied, after a moment's pause.

Westermann waited for the low chuckle around the room to die down. "So we're being watched, as we're watching them. But you said no life signs, so likely a satellite of some sort, gathering information of the planet." He paused a beat. "Human? Qoearc? Or something else?"

"The latter, most likely, Captain. Configuration matches no known human or Qoearc design."

"If crewed," said Hamilton, moving closer to stand behind Westermann, "approximate number?"

Sh'zaoqoq contemplated the question. "Perhaps fifty or sixty, assuming mass and size that of our typical norms."

"Science station, therefore," said Xiaoli. "Too small for a military outpost or something permanent. Perhaps left running for later return."

"How long ago?" asked Westermann, the explorer in him becoming more curious by the minute.

"No answers yet, Captain. However, Commander Xiaoli and I both recommend careful approach."

Westermann nodded. "Agreed. But approach we shall. Earthfleet's mission is exploration, and this is two discoveries, not one; a new planet and possibly a new species." He looked around the room, noting anxiousness beginning to show in many faces. "Let's get to it".

* * *

The station continued its observations. Now that the object was closer, it could detect signs of life within, though like nothing it had seen before. The vessel, for that is now what it appeared to be, was larger than any previously recorded, propelled by titanic forces driving it through the "other space", away from the material universe, and capable of speeds unheard of. If the crew of the vessel knew how much information the station was collecting, they likely would have been concerned.

The station was fascinated. How to learn more of these seemingly magic abilities. It brought more power online, reconfigured sensors, hid probing frequencies in the general background radiation of the system's star. Whatever it could learn must be done before the vessel arrived.

Still, however, the station only waited. Even though the vessel approached quickly, it showed no sign of malevolence. No changes in energy output, such as weapons would indicate. Only minimal sensing detected. That would likely change as it drew closer. As for weapons, the station quickly determined, based on the energy output of the vessel, its own defenses would be ineffective in a battle. Therefore, it made adjustments for protection, should it become necessary, and prepared to launch a buoy with findings to its creator's location before the vessel got too much closer.

In the meantime, it only tracked, recorded, and analyzed. And wondered. How would this species react to the station itself? Would they attempt to strip its knowledge, claim the planet below as its own, then destroy the station? Would they occupy the station and attempt to hold it from those who built it? And what of this strange time difference it noted, as the vessel neared?

These were logical questions. Therefore, the station began to prepare logical responses… just in case.

Two
Standard Orbit

"Duty Log, Captain Noah Westermann, 030217.10. We're about to enter the system of the planet around which is orbiting a very mysterious space station. Tactical, Sciences, and Engineering are all spending hours analyzing our scans as systems normalize and we draw closer. And the station itself is watching us very covertly. It will be interesting to see if it's crewed and simply shielded, or an autonomous construct. Regardless, we'll know soon... and hope the Qoearc haven't followed to interrupt our investigation."

* * *

EAS Agincourt...

Agincourt dropped from hyperlight twelve hours from the star's singularity border. Hyperlight travel was not possible inside that boundary, as the curvature of space was far too severe. Experiments with unmanned probes, during the early days of hyperlight travel, had proven so; ships entering the stars' sphere of gravitational influence, while in hyperlight, simply disappeared, never to be seen again. Many theories had been postulated; the probes entered a wormhole, emerging in another dimension or place and time; the probes stayed in the energetic hyperlight state and never could return, due to gravitational limitations and forces keeping them there; or the probes simply were destroyed. Regardless, accidents had happened on more than one occasion. And Noah Westermann had no intention of being the most recent.

"Secure from hyperlight, Ms. Maddani, put us in a polar orbit. Mister Butler, give the Conn a program that will allow us to map the entire planet in minimum time."

Westermann turned to the Science console. "Status on the station?"

Xiaoli stepped from her chair to the captain's side, PADD in hand. "Scans have increased but still passive only. There appears to be no shielding preventing our sensors from penetrating the station's hull, and it is similar to our duranium in composition. The interior is divided into many chambers and rooms. I have a general schematic if you would care to see it."

Westermann nodded. "On screen two." *Agincourt*, as all newer ships, was equipped with two programmable viewing screens. The left one lit, showing a three-dimensional representation of the station. Levels and floors showed in various colors, with a legend to one side.

"Here and here, observation posts," said Xiaoli, laser pointer in hand. "This level appears to be a science lab, this one the computer core. Two levels below are quarters, and from what we can see, the inhabitants were smaller in stature than typical human norm. Approximately one and one-half meters tall, certainly no more."

"Crew complement?"

"One hundred ten, sir. Even for so small a crew, the station is very compact. We estimate the total volume to be no more than three thousand cubic meters."

"People would get very friendly," quipped Butler from the Nav station.

Westermann showed a wan smile. "Continue, Commander."

"The planet as noted previously is extremely early Earth-like. No higher lifeforms, very young in development, perhaps three billion years, no more. Vegetation covers nearly two-thirds of the planet and is dense. Mountains are all young, seas show light salinity throughout. Currents are strong around the two major continents, lesser around three smaller. There is a single moon, about two thousand kilometers in diameter, which accounts for the tides and currents."

"Shore leave," said Butler, turning to Westermann. "When can we debark, Captain?" He showed a grin.

Westermann chuckled. "You can stay at the Nav station, Lieutenant, and make sure we maintain stable orbit. Very well, Commander, return to your station. Tactical, report on the Qoearc, if you have one."

Sh'zaoqoq swiveled in her chair. "We were not followed, and I have no further information regarding the Qoearc' status or location, sir."

Lori Hamilton stepped onto the Bridge as the Tactical Officer gave her report. "Check this system thoroughly. We don't want any surprises."

Sh'zaoqoq looked to Westermann, who nodded. "Proceed. Give me a report as soon as you've completed your scan." The captain glanced to Hamilton, now standing at his side. "Good morning." He noted the coffee cup in her hands. "Have you made your rounds?"

"Just finished in Engineering, heading for Sickbay in a minute. Hyperlight power is up to ninety percent, environmental stable, accumulators are fully charged. We have weapons in case we need them." She motioned to the planet. "Beautiful. Unspoiled. Where are we, exactly?"

Butler turned in his chair. "Free space, Commander. We're about five light years outside Earth Alliance exploration, three light years from the closest Qoearc outpost, and a couple of light years from a Stiz colony."

"Stiz?" Westermann shot a glance to his navigator. "Why didn't you inform me of this earlier? Stiz are known hostiles to Earthfleet."

Butler opened his mouth, but no words emerged. At last he managed to speak. "I… had not filed my daily report yet, sir, but was going to include it. I'll do so now." He turned back to his console, chagrined.

Westermann held his temper but looked sternly to Hamilton. She nodded. "Understood. We'll take care of it."

"Captain, I have new information regarding the station." Xiaoli spoke from the Science console, continuing as Westermann nodded to her. "Scans have increased. I'm also detecting some previously unnoticed time-signatures. All very… fascinating."

"Elaborate, please."

Xiaoli once again watched the displays on her screens scrolling quickly by. "Difficult to explain or analyze. Please allow me a bit of time."

"Do you need additional resources?" asked Hamilton.

"Tactical sensors would be helpful, yes." Xiaoli looked to Sh'zaoqoq who quickly ran her hands over the controls.

"Patched in now, Commander."

Xiaoli continued her scan as the Bridge grew quiet, waiting. At last she turned to Westermann. "Captain, I have no explanation for what I'm seeing. There are strong indications of time flowing in a different manner aboard the station, but I cannot confirm without…"

"Without what, Commander?" asked Hamilton, trading glances with the captain.

"Request permission to assemble a landing party and board the station to investigate. This is unprecedented, sir."

Westermann shook his head. "Denied… for the moment. Continue your analysis and prepare a report before the end of your duty shift. Commander Hamilton will assist, and you can set up a team in the astrolab for further study."

Hamilton motioned to the lift. "Commander, come with me. We'll work together on this."

They took their exit through the doors quickly. Westermann gave a look to Tactical, then the Nav station. "Lieutenant Butler, assist Commander Sh'zaoqoq and get me all the information you have on the Stiz whereabouts. I need it now."

* * *

The vessel was here! It had appeared in normal space beyond the star's gravitational pull, to within ninety-nine point nine nine percent. Surely this meant the "other space" propulsion would not operate within a gravity well. Or perhaps gravity acted adversely on the vessel if it attempted to do so. It might even cause its destruction. The station filed the information for further study.

The vessel assumed orbit about the planet, crossing the poles, obviously to map the planet's surface. Therefore, the crew was interested in the planet, for resources or colonization or simply out of curiosity, the station could not know at this point. More questions to seek answers to later.

It took the opportunity to study the vessel more closely. The hull was similar in construction to the station's own, but denser and thicker. Instrumentation was everywhere, not in antennae or pods as on the station, but in well-protected and concealed areas in strategic locations around the hull. Except for the large semi-disc, deep in a well-like enclosure in the underneath part of the ship. And somewhat vulnerable. Again, the station made note and filed the information.

But so much room! And occupied by less than five hundred life-forms. They were larger than the creators by about thirty percent. They moved more slowly, almost lethargically, compared to those who had crewed the station. The time-signatures were… strange. The station came to a decision; increase scanning power. A chance, surely, but the crew of the vessel would certainly be aware by now the station was watching them as they observed it. Even if they did appear to be moving in time differently.

Was this done purposely? Did the vessel's crew have power over the flow of time?

As did the station's creators?

* * *

Abol Ch'virrorh took time in Engineering to review *Agincourt's* repairs with his Tec-Staff and confirm everything was "ship-shape", as Captain Westermann liked to say. Once complete, and following twelve standard hours of duty and crawling through the power core after cooldown, he found his way to quarters, hoping for a real shower of hot water, some meditation, and sleep, for the first time in nearly a full day. What he found, as his bondmates would say, was welcome as *challorn*, an Arneci sweet-smelling flower.

Thevoss stood at the shower room entrance, draped in a heavy robe. She glowed. Her eyes, those near-black orbs of depth, shone as onyx. She smirked. "Cleanse yourself, as you stink of grease and sweat. I will not have you in my bed otherwise."

Abol drew closer, laid his forehead to hers, and lightly touched her face. They stayed that way for moments, no words necessary, hands entwined at their sides, eyes closed, sharing breath between them.

Abol drew back slowly. "You are well? I cannot keep my mind from you, and worry every hour. Now we face danger and unknown."

Thevoss studied him closely. "I am hardly the first

female Arnec to carry a child. My mind says I know the way of this." She showed a smile again.

"Our bondmates on the Base have been advised, yes? You know we will be reassigned once we return. It may mean the end of our shipboard careers. Arnec ministers may require our repatriation."

"We may be slowed in our careers, but not stopped. With a child, would Fleet Base Twelve be such an unwelcome thing? Do you wish to chase our child through the phase coils and down the catwalks?" Thevoss grinned.

Abol didn't return her smile. "We should think carefully about this. Arnec would be the best place for us until the birth. Safety first, yes?"

"The best minds on Arnec and of Earth Alliance seek a solution for this. There is no shame in how the universe proceeds, and this is not retribution. Abol, I worry of your preoccupation on this matter. I am well. I am alive. I am happy."

He closed his eyes, as if in solemn agreement. "Your words are heard and honored. You state your position eloquently as always you do. You carry our child as part of the Arneci future. Your will is mine."

They touched foreheads softly once again and held each other. "I will clean myself as asked." He glanced to the shower room. "Would you join me?"

"I have showered and must return to duty soon. However…" Thevoss grinned. "That does not mean I cannot assist as you need."

* * *

The intercom on Westermann's command seat buzzed. "Bridge."

"Xiaoli, Captain. We have information regarding the station for your review."

"Bring it to my ready room." Westermann closed the switch and rose. "Ms. Maddani, you have the Conn. Commander Sh'zaoqoq, finalize your report regarding the Stiz and bring it to my ready room as soon as possible." He disappeared through the doors before anyone could respond.

Xiaoli and Hamilton arrived minutes later. The XO activated the wall screen after a nod from Westermann. "Captain, we have made some astounding observations. The time-flow aboard the station appears to be backward from our own."

Westermann exchanged glances with Hamilton, then spoke. "Explain, please. I'm not sure I follow."

Xiaoli brought a schematic up on the screen. "In our universe, time flows as a constant in one direction; that of entropy increasing. We have found 'pockets' of time moving in different ways, and those are in Earthfleet and Alliance records. There are theories, some postulated by the Terran Science Academy, that time has a 'polarity', such as a magnet possesses. And under certain circumstances, the polarity may be reversed, either by artificial means or natural causes."

"What sort of artificial means would be required to do so, Commander?" asked Westermann, shaking his head.

Hamilton spoke before Xiaoli could continue. "We're not certain of the mechanism, but our studies show something very odd is happening on the station. Whether this is truly a reverse flow of time or some sort of screen or masking for security, it comes down to this; the station exists only in part in our universe."

"What would happen if we boarded the station to study

this phenomenon?"

Xiaoli shook her head. "Unknown, Captain. Our scans are disrupted by the reverse time-flow as we apply more power. We postulate possible harm to life such as ours, not to mention unknown effects upon the station itself."

The door hail sounded. "Come in," said Westermann, and Sh'zaoqoq and Butler entered quietly. "Commander, repeat your findings, please."

As Xiaoli explained, Westermann once more met Hamilton's eyes. She nodded knowingly. "We'll find out what's going on," she said softly.

Xiaoli completed her review, then turned again to the captain. "Further information, sir. The station continues to scan us, but we have blocked most of the sensors. Still, we're certain there is a very sophisticated AI operating the station. At least equivalent to Base intelligence and perhaps more. It seems to be adapting to our attempts to keep our secrets."

"Secrets only because we don't know what this station will do," added Hamilton. "We are learning much of it as well, and in my opinion, Captain, this discovery is as important as the planet itself."

"What of the planet?" asked Butler. "As good as it looks?"

"A fair question," replied Xiaoli. "The oceans are filled with life, some quite developed. No significant land life beyond small mammal-like creatures and massive vegetation as noted previously. The air is clean, water plentiful, and environment stable and typically Earth-like. A wealth of resources and certainly a potential colony planet."

The room was quiet for moments as Westermann considered all the implications of the station, the planet, and the possibility of known adversaries in the neighborhood.

"Commander Sh'zaoqoq, your report, please."

The Arneci woman motioned to Butler, who showed a nervous grin. "If I may, sir." He pointed to the screen and Westermann nodded. The picture changed to a schematic of the star's vicinity. "There is a known Stiz outpost about two and one-half light years from here. It's in free space, but knowing the Stiz, anywhere they are, they consider their territory.

"The closest Qoearc world is nearly ten light years away, but there are a couple of small border stations on rocks with a very long orbit around neighboring stars. The Qoearc move these from time to time, to keep our outposts in view. We also know they've had more than one run-in with the Stiz."

Westermann nodded, traded glances with his Tactical Officer, then looked back to Butler. "Recommendations regarding the Stiz?"

Butler shrugged. "Keep an eye out for their ships. Likely they patrol systems close by. This one wouldn't be any use to them, and unless there is a planet closer to the star with higher temps and a more suitable environment for their kind, I don't see any reason they would bother us."

"Except that we are here," said Sh'zaoqoq. "Tactics require a consideration of what an enemy can do, not necessarily what they might do. Threat estimates regarding Stiz encounters are quite high, Lieutenant."

Westermann nearly grinned, then looked once more to Xiaoli. "What about counteracting this time-flow issue if we decide to board the station? And how would we communicate with a landing party?"

She considered for a moment. "I can't be certain, but a physical object from our universe entering into one that is possibly anchored in another universe may be difficult, but not impossible. Perhaps we might find a way to minimize the time-flow or neutralize it in a localized area."

"Such as an environmental suit?" asked Hamilton. "Can such a device be small enough to carry in a backpack or pouch?"

"Unknown, Commander. However, we'll do some testing and find out."

Westermann nodded. "Do so. Requisition whatever resources you need." He looked to Butler. "The Lieutenant will assist you as well. And prepare a list for a possible visit to the station."

"What of the planet, Captain?" asked Hamilton.

"One thing at a time, Commander. If this station is in a reverse time-flow, it might disappear at any moment. If it has secrets beneficial to the Alliance or Earthfleet, we may want to learn those."

"The station is the property of others, Captain," said Hamilton carefully. "Beings we know nothing of and who may return at any moment."

"Agreed, and by going aboard the station, we can learn about them as well. Get some answers on this time-flow issue and let me know what you can do to neutralize it, or possibly mask us from it. We have an opportunity. Let's not waste it."

* * *

Westermann was in the officers' mess when text appeared on his PADD again.

WE NEED TO TALK. XO

I can't get away from that woman, he thought, and typed a reply. I'M IN THE MESS. COME ON DOWN AND HAVE A CUP OF COFFEE.

Hamilton appeared moments later as the captain placed his utensils in the recycler. He drew two cups and set them on the table.

"Here to read me the riot act again?" Westermann smiled.

"No sir. Only a word or two of caution." Hamilton drank slowly, then continued. "This has echoes of what happened at the pulsar system."

"You mean because I'm considering sending a party to a station we know little about, but may hold magic we can't even comprehend?"

Hamilton sighed. "Something like that, yes."

Westermann waited for more, but the XO was silent. "Do you know why you'll never be captain, Commander? You lack curiosity of the unknown and your natural caution gets in the way sometimes."

"On the contrary, sir, I have enormous curiosity about the universe and all that's in it."

Westermann nodded. "You have the scientific curiosity, yes, and you do it well. You bring out the best in others who have that same type of curiosity, such as Xiaoli. But you're afraid to step outside your front door when the time comes to do so."

Hamilton looked away, a frown on her face. At last she turned to Westermann again. "I'm sorry to hear you say that, sir. I thought you brought me on board because you approved of my performance."

"I do, most assuredly. You have a wonderful way with the crew I don't have, that your former CO didn't appreciate. If I hadn't asked for you, you might have ended up behind a desk, and I didn't want to see that. You have too much to offer to a crew… and a captain who sorely needs your talents."

She sipped, the showed a wan smile. "You do lack a bit of, shall we say, personality, with others from time to time, sir. But only from time to time."

He nodded. "Okay, now that that's out of the way, what's the real issue? Give me solid reasons for not sending a team."

"I won't try to dissuade you, sir. Rather, let me lead the team. That way my natural caution, as you call it, can control the exuberance the landing party is sure to feel. I don't disagree this is something we must investigate, but at the same time, while salvage laws might generally apply, this is a functioning artifact, an AI the likes of which we've never encountered, and we don't want to make it mad. We have yet to determine if it even has any weapon systems, and there are certainly none we've detected. But the builders of this remarkable station can't have left it undefended."

Westermann considered as he poured more coffee for them both. "Very well, and good points, too. Who's on the team?"

Hamilton bought up her PADD. "Xiaoli, Butler for experience. He's got a good mind, but very young still. I'd like to take Chief Abol for engineering issues. Arneci are great at spotting things we humans miss. Two S-Techs, preferably with exo-biology training, an E-Tech for Abol, and a couple of security guards, just in case. And me."

"Sounds good. What about Commander Sh'zaoqoq?"

Hamilton nodded after a moment. "For tactical considerations, you mean? Look for weapons or defensive systems?"

"That… and to keep her calm while her bondmate is off-ship. You know she's carrying a child, right?"

"Yes, sir. And I agree, but with the typical reservations. Chief Abol can probably spot anything she can."

"She can keep them both calm in doing so. Plan on no more than ten hours per visit, and she can go on the first one to see there's no imminent danger to Abol. I need her back on board to keep track of the Stiz and Qoearc, in case they're still lurking about. Hopefully we can gather all the information we need in three or four days. In the meantime, Nav and Sciences will continue mapping the planet. They can try out that new cartography program they've been raving about."

"Aye, sir. Anything else?"

"Be careful. Use that natural caution. It's worked very well for us over the last couple of years and I don't want you to misplace it."

Hamilton grinned. "I'll take that as a compliment, sir."

Westermann nodded. "As I intended. Let's get to work."

* * *

The station sensed the small craft approaching and watched as it carefully docked in an open port. The port had purposely been left available, to see if the crew had the curiosity to come aboard. The station also wondered still of the time-flow differences, and how these strange, slow creatures would deal with it. Or if they would risk existing in it, to see what might happen.

Their solution was simple and eloquent. The creatures carried stasis generators, which projected a deep-bluish glow around each one. Presumably this was only a visual que, to confirm to the creatures the field was working, for the effect itself had no color component to the frequency. This stasis field simply separated the creatures themselves from the station's time-flow; no interference on either side, no harm done to the station or the creatures. The station made a note; these creatures were clever and intelligent, and might be more of a concern than originally thought.

In the meantime, as the small craft docked and the crew made their way slowly about the hangar and into the lock, the station turned much of its processing power to the large vessel itself, and the myriad of secrets slowly being uncovered. The station was therefore busy, busier than it had been since the creators left. This gave a sense of purpose and of accomplishment to the station, knowing it was fulfilling its orders and directives.

Circuits hummed with power, processing units recorded, analyzed, sorted, and picked apart each datum as it was gathered. Heat sinks glowed and logic pathways glistened with energy, sensors sensed, and monitors monitored. In all, it was a time of extreme input and productivity.

A human might have referred to this feeling as happiness.

Three
Hostage Situation

"Duty Log, Captain Noah Westermann, 030417.02. The landing party has spent the better part of two days aboard the alien station with no major issues. In the meantime, we continue to map the planet and I'm considering a landing party there as well, but at the moment, it's not a priority. Besides, if the Stiz or Qoearc show up, I don't want to have to retrieve crew from two sites. Therefore, Agincourt is maintaining a high polar orbit, to expedite the survey process. Commander Hamilton's team will return to the ship in the next couple of hours for rest and debriefing."

* * *

The Station…

It had taken the landing party a full shift to get their investigations headed in the right direction. Hamilton insisted on a refuge bubble being set up first thing in the docking port, with a stasis generator enclosing it. In an emergency, they could all retreat to the bubble and be assured the time-flow issues, which were still not fully understood, would not affect them. How they might then get to the shuttle hadn't been determined, but at least they would be temporarily safe. Later shifts were confined to investigations of the lock and nearby corridors.

They found the station cramped as had been thought. The observation deck, at the top of the station, had a two-meter ceiling height. With insulated boots and full environmental helmets, nearly all the party had to crouch most of the time. Only the center area of the observation platform, with its peaked ceiling, allowed them to stand fully upright. Needless to say, backaches were common, and the middle of the deck was where they congregated often for discussions. Lighter than Earth-normal gravity also helped.

The station itself was a marvel of simplicity. Instruments were mostly touch panels, obviously made for hands smaller than human-standard. Abol and his E-Tech traced the systems to the main power source which, itself, was as compact as any he had ever seen. The station seemed to run on a tapping of the universal vacuum, something only the best of Earth Alliance scientists understood to any degree. The team spent as much time as possible working to carefully uncover its mysteries. Very carefully. The energy potential was nearly incalculable, the Chief Engineer had told Hamilton during a private consultation.

"I cannot disassemble anything, Commander, and for various reasons. Firstly, the panel enclosing the power source is one piece of material, a seamless ceramic that will not pass a current. Therefore, our scans cannot penetrate it and we cannot know its operating methods. The whole of the assembly weighs only some three hundred kilos, as far as we can estimate. I am most impressed by this species' engineering acumen."

"Leave it alone, Abol, it doesn't belong to us anyway. Do what you can; vids, notes, anything. Include whatever you can learn indirectly by how much current is drawn by the systems it's powering. We're not taking it home with us." Hamilton grinned, then motioned to Sh'zaoqoq, PADD in hand, examining a vertical instrument panel of blank displays. "Is your bondmate well? She seems to be intrigued as the rest of us."

"She is an intellect as few others. I have said many times she has the mind of a scientist, not a weapons-wielder. Our thanks for allowing us to examine this wonder of engineering together."

"We need to wrap up this session and head back to *Agincourt*. See to it, please, Chief, and I'll get the shuttle warmed up."

Hamilton headed for the hatchway to the docking port as Abol set about completing his assignment and preparing the landing party to leave. As the First Officer approached the hatch, an audible click came from the mechanism within, and the X-shaped hand lever rotated half a turn. Hamilton stopped, watching carefully. She looked about; no one else had noticed the peculiarity as it occurred. She waited a moment, then took the lever in hand and tried to turn it. It wouldn't move. She put more effort into it, but again, the lever stayed in place.

"Chief… Ensign Monroe." She motioned to Abol and the security guard he was speaking to. "Try the lever, please. It appears to be stuck."

"Allow me, sir." Monroe, a lanky young human male, tried the lever once, then twice. The third time, he put serious muscle to it with no success.

Abol ran his scanner over the lever, then the hatch itself. "Locked, Commander. This was not so only a few minutes ago when we moved a new audio analyzer into the observation deck."

"Check the mechanism on the left," said Hamilton. "That's where I heard the sound from."

Abol again scanned the area. By now, the entire party had assembled around them, except for the Science Techs in the crew quarters and the security guard with them. "Confirmed. The energy output has changed and is now polarized in the opposite direction. We are locked in."

Hamilton passed her gaze about the assembled crew. "Did anyone touch any controls? Maybe brushed against something unbeknownst? Change any settings on any of the instruments or panels?"

The crew looked to each other, all shaking their heads. Sh'zaoqoq spoke. "Commander, I recorded a minor change in energy output a moment before you tried the lever. In this panel." She pointed to a set of screens to one side. Where they had been blank, now all were showing wave patterns of unknown meaning.

"Alright." Hamilton motioned for the crew to back away from the hatch. "Mister Butler, contact the S-Techs and let me know their status. Chief Abol, get me as much information on this latching mechanism as you can, quickly. Xiaoli, assist Commander Sh'zaoqoq with an assessment of our equipment and supplies, as well as a rundown on everyone's suit status and battery reserve." She moved aside and pressed her communicator button. "*Agincourt*, this is Commander Hamilton. Indigo Status."

"Receiving, Commander, patching you through to the Captain. Stand by."

Hamilton looked at her chronometer. The captain was likely in quarters or in the mess. She waited, calming herself as she could. They were in serious trouble, and she knew it, but had to keep the crew busy.

"Westermann." The captain's voice was slow, and she knew he had been sleeping.

"Sir, we have a problem."

"A moment, Commander."

Again, Hamilton waited, knowing Westermann was likely washing the sleep from his eyes. Sleep that might be the last he would have for a while, should things become serious.

"Alright, go ahead."

"Sir, the station has locked us in the observation deck. I

can't say this is purposeful, as nothing else has changed. We may be seeing only a safety protocol we're not aware of." She glanced to Butler, now standing at her side. He shook his head. "The S-Techs are also locked in the station crew quarters, so there's a pattern. Again, no hostile moves, and it may be a simple lock-down procedure."

"And it may not, Commander. Very well. Party status?"

"All accounted for, suits are all at maximum integrity, stasis fields operating normally. But our refuge is in the hangar, so I'm going to order minimum power on the suits and sleep for everyone, if things don't change quickly."

"Agreed. Are the observation ports still clear? You can see out, we could see in, correct?"

Hamilton understood the question. If *Agincourt* had to break in, the ports would be the weakest areas.

"Yes, sir, we can see the planet below clearly. Also, no movement outside the station at this time." *No big mechanical claws coming to grab us,* she though, a sardonic smile in her mind.

"Other exits?"

Hamilton considered. Surely there was an emergency hatch somewhere in the main deck. The floor, perhaps. "We'll check immediately, sir, and advise. In the meantime, my thought is, comm would be the next thing to go. So we'll prepare something else in case that's the station's plan."

"The station? Is this a possibility, Lori?"

She shrugged. "Who else? The station is empty of life except for us. Surely it knows we're here and is observing. Maybe it decided to collect specimens."

The line was quiet for a time. "Sir?"

"Still here, just thinking. Alright, report back in thirty minutes if things haven't changed. I'll order a course change to

bring us to the station's vicinity."

"Aye, sir. We'll contact *Agincourt* again in thirty minutes. Hamilton out." She pressed the button again, turned and faced the crew, now gathered and listening. "Okay, ladies and gentlemen, let's find out what's going on here. Everything you can tell me in the next twenty-five minutes. Commander Sh'zaoqoq, you and Mister Butler will please find us a way out of here. Through the decking if necessary, but find a way."

* * *

EAS Agincourt...

Westermann alerted the Bridge and gave orders from the sonic shower. *Agincourt* broke polar orbit and quickly coasted into position ten kilometers from the alien station as he dressed and headed for the Bridge.

He entered and took the command seat, looking to unfamiliar faces at Tactical and Sciences. "Status!"

"Standby Alert as ordered, Captain. All weapons and shields are charged. Awaiting your further commands."

"Lieutenant Phillips, isn't it? Very well, maintain Alert, keep your eye out for any other ships entering the system. We don't want to be surprised by something else while this matter is ongoing. Sciences?"

"No change, sir, only minor fluctuations in the station's energy output, the time-flow effect is still in and around the station itself. The field encompasses an area about one hundred meters beyond the station proper."

"Monitor and set an alarm for any changes. Comm, do we have a secure channel to the station?"

"Yes sir, no interruption at this time."

"Engineering?"

"Board is green, sir, full power available, accumulators at maximum."

"Helm, Nav?"

"Helm is answering, sir, Nav screens are clear."

Westermann glanced at the chronometer in his chair arm. Ten minutes before the next contact. He punched the intercom button. "Sickbay, Bridge. Doctor Kamisori, please come up here for a bit, I need your expertise." He closed the circuit. "Tactical, give me an analysis of the clear material in the observation ports of the station. How much energy would be required to cut through it, if necessary."

Phillips scanned his instruments and watched the display. "It's similar to our standard transparent ballistic armor, sir, but a bit denser. Hand torches wouldn't touch it, assault weapons would probably do the job, but take minutes for full penetration. I don't recommend using PAKS."

"What if we cut to one one-hundredth power?"

Phillips quickly ran through his calculations. "That would pretty much vaporize the material in two or three seconds, sir. Debris outgassing would likely be a problem."

"That's what I want." Westermann pressed the intercom button again. "Security, Bridge."

"Mayfield here, sir."

"Lieutenant, get two squads to assault shuttles on the double. Launch when ready and take up positions around the station where you have a clear shot at the observation ports. Confirm when you're on station. Do not fire without my direct order." He clicked off and looked at the chronometer again. Five minutes.

* * *

The station observed and recorded the events with growing interest. With no malice, it was intent on testing these creatures, to determine if they might be dangerous to the station, and therefore, those who created it. With the simple solution to the time-flow issue solved, it reasoned other problems might be overcome just as quickly. Therefore, it put a simple test before them, one not only to place the creatures in a physically isolated state from part of their number, but to see how quickly they might resolve it.

The station was not surprised that in a short time, they had discovered the secondary hatchway behind a panel, and the access there to rooms below. However, it also came to notice the creature leading others down the stairwell carried an object in its forehand; not a scanning device or sensor, but a weapon. Certainly, one of limited power and ability, but a weapon, nonetheless. This called up additional alarms, subroutines, and protocols. The station's programming included such redundancies, in case, by some unusual circumstance, it might be boarded by hostiles. While at the time the creatures showed no intent of the sort, the possibility now was there, and the station would react accordingly. If the weapon could be neutralized, that was acceptable. If not, then the wielder would be neutralized, by whatever means necessary.

Again, no malice was intended, yet the station had its orders. Orders that overrode even its own curiosity to "investigate new life". Here, the life had come to it, but now the rules had changed. The station prepared as programming required, and would take whatever actions it might, at the appropriate time. Time that was approaching quickly.

* * *

The Station…

Security Ensign Monroe led the way down. The steps were narrow, short, and clumsy to take too fast. His boot heels caught on the step above, and he had to steady himself against the wall. The passage was hardly wide enough for him to make his way through without turning sideways. In all, it made keeping his hand weapon aimed ahead while descending difficult.

"Hold your position, Ensign." Hamilton called from behind as she trailed Monroe, the E-Tech Hardy, and Chief Abol. The hatchway to the next level lay before them, and she wanted a moment to think things through before they opened it. Or tried.

"Chief, run your scanner over the hatch and mechanism. I don't want to touch something running an active current."

Abol held his scanner over Monroe's head, watching the flickering display. "No current, and the polarity is as the upper hatch before it locked, Commander."

Hamilton nodded. "Keep your scanner running. Ensign, proceed."

Monroe took the cross-shaped lever in one hand, his weapon still in the other. The moment he began to turn the lever, he yelped and fell back, nearly knocking the E-Tech over. Monroe held his left hand, grimacing. His side arm smoldered on the flooring.

"Back off, now!" Hamilton retreated, fast as she could go without falling on everyone below her. They reached the observation deck and closed the hatch. Sh'zaoqoq came forward quickly, spraying the ensign's hand and wrist with numbing salve, and wrapped it quickly with a bandage. She looked to Abol, who only shook his head, then turned to Hamilton. "The current flow began only as the ensign touched the lever. It was not present before."

Hamilton nodded. "Therefore, he was attacked. Might it be because he held a weapon? Is this AI perceptive enough it can recognize such?"

Sh'zaoqoq spoke when the others remained silent. "Unknown. Regardless, we must assume intent was to disarm, but not kill. There is only one sure way to test the theory, and that is to try again."

"I will go," said Abol.

"Denied," replied Hamilton. "Let's think this through a bit more. Mister Butler, contact the S-Techs below and confirm they're still alright. I need to call the ship." She moved away as the others congregated once again in the center of the chamber, talking quietly among themselves. "*Agincourt*, Hamilton, checking in per previous communique. Please put Captain Westermann on the line."

"Agincourt, Commander, please stand by."

Hamilton watched the crew quietly. Butler signaled a thumbs-up and she nodded.

"Westermann. Report, Commander."

"More issues, sir. The station made an open attack on Security Ensign Monroe as we descended the stair below. Nothing serious, but it purposely disabled the weapon in his hand. We're considering trying it again without showing weapons."

"Everyone else safe? The crew below?"

"Yes, sir, no other attacks or injuries."

"Have those below ascend to your location. Get everyone together. Find a way to the hangar deck and prepare to disembark."

Hamilton paused before she answered. "Understood, sir, but I recommend we stay to complete this shift. In the meantime, I'll have Chief Abol and his E-Tech work through the problem of getting to the hangar. The crew needs to stay busy. Tension is getting a bit thick."

"Very well. And if you'll look out the windows, you'll see two assault shuttles in place. If need arises, we can take out the viewports and get everyone out that way."

"I saw them earlier, sir. I hope it doesn't come to that, but this station is beginning to show signs of a very inquisitive AI. And my opinion is, it will continue to test us as long as we're here."

"Agreed. Proceed, Commander, and check back in thirty minutes."

"Aye, sir. Hamilton out." She clicked the switch and sighed. Their investigation had just become a bit more urgent, and knowing the captain, he wouldn't hesitate to get them out in whatever way necessary.

* * *

EAS Agincourt…

Westermann called Sickbay again, Dr. Kamisori having not responded to his previous call. One of the nurses answered.

"The doctor was off-duty, sir. She stood three watches in a row. Apologies for not getting back to you sooner."

"Why was the doctor on duty for eighteen hours?"

"We're getting cases in of… well, motion sickness. General dizziness, nausea, ringing in the ears, that sort of thing."

"How many?"

"About thirty, sir, and they're all coming from the outer areas of the ship. Dr. Kamisori is of the opinion the time-flow issues may be causing them."

Westermann bit back a rebuke. *And she didn't think it important to tell me, with the landing party on the ship?* He counted to ten before continuing. "Where is the doctor now?"

A pause on the intercom, then Kamisori's voice came through. *"Yes, Captain, what can I do for you?"*

"Review the recent records from the party onboard the station. I need your expertise as to how long they can hold up under these circumstances." *Then you and I will have a talk about respect for command,* he thought.

"Captain, I scanned them as they came in just now. If you're asking about psychological issues regarding the time-flow, I have no idea. We've never encountered anything like this and there is nothing in Earthfleet or Alliance records I can find. But you heard my nurse tell you about concerns for the crew and the physical issues they are manifesting." She paused. *"You do understand the implications, correct?"*

Westermann began to speak, then shook his head. "Explain, Doctor, we may not have a lot of time."

"I'm not a physicist, but as it was explained to me by one of my nurses who is a hobbyist, since the time-flow is the reverse of ours, this station may be waiting for the planet to return to its formation. However long that may be."

"Commander Xiaoli reported the planet is over three billion years old, Doctor."

"Yes, I attended the briefing remotely. So the station may be designed to stay until the planet, in the station's time frame, returns to its formative state."

Westermann conceded. "No, it was not discussed. Why would this occur to your nurse?"

Kamisori chuckled. *"She's a hobbyist, like I said. Sometimes those with less formal training see things differently. It's just a theory. But it has other implications."*

"Go on."

"It implies the station was assembled at some point back in time as we know it. How long ago, there is likely no way to

determine."

"So… the station could disassemble itself at some time in… our future. Soon?"

"Again, a theory, Captain. She's been talking about this since we arrived."

"And what might alert us to this?"

Again, Kamisori laughed. *"If the station starts taking itself apart, it's probably a bad sign."*

Westermann closed his eyes, wishing his social skills were better with the recalcitrant doctor. "Very well. Give my thanks to your nurse for her insight. Westermann out." He snapped the switch savagely, glaring at the screen. *Dammit. Dammit!*

* * *

The Station…

The S-Techs and security ensign appeared through the floor hatchway with no delays. Hamilton reasoned it had been the brandished side arm that set off the station's defense programming, and ordered all weapons holstered and powered-down. Chief Abol had traced the circuitry keeping the hatch to the hangar locked and confirmed he could override it, with a bit of luck.

"Luck?" Hamilton grinned at the engineer. "I thought it was the 'passion of the hunt' that the Arneci used as explanation of success. Now it's luck?"

Abol nodded slowly, his dark eyes nearly invisible behind the helmet visor. "Too much time around humans, Commander, and I have learned poor habits. My apologies." He grinned.

"Prepare immediately, so we can get out of here. I'm sure Captain Westermann is anxious to get us all back aboard *Agincourt.*"

"Yes, Commander." He moved to the hatch once more, where he was joined by Sh'zaoqoq.

"Not a situation we were expecting," she said, moving closer.

Abol watched his scanner for a moment, then turned to face her. "We will return safely, once this hatch is unsealed." He watched her face carefully. "You appear pale. Speak of it."

She looked away. Perspiration grew on her forehead, and her eyes were half-closed. "Truly, I am very tired. I worry, too..."

"For the child?" Abol raised his face. "Commander, there is a problem!"

Hamilton came to his side immediately. Thevoss leaned against her, knees sagging. "Lay her down, quickly. Xiaoli, your medical scanner please."

Xiaoli knelt and passed the scanner over Thevoss's prone figure. "Heart rate elevated, temperature as well, brain activity below optimum and slowing."

"What does this mean?" Abol took his bondmate's hand and looked to the science officer.

"Unknown, but not a good sign. I recommend immediate return to *Agincourt*, Commander."

Hamilton touched the intercom button on her suit sleeve. "*Agincourt*, Hamilton. Medical emergency, get Doctor Kamisori on the line!"

They waited as Xiaoli scanned Thevoss once again. "Stable, but not strong. Medical attention is needed."

"Stay strong," said Abol to Thevoss in Arneci. *"This will pass, and you will be stronger for it."*

"Kamisori here. What's the problem, Commander?"

Hamilton nodded to Xiaoli, who repeated her findings. There was a pause as they waited for the ship to respond.

"Alright, it's likely something to do with the time-flow and her pregnancy. Get her back to the ship as quickly as possible. You're all wearing stasis gear, correct?"

"Affirmative, Doctor," replied Xiaoli, before Hamilton could answer."

"Good. Put her in immediate suspension. That will stop any further degeneration and give us time."

"Do it," Hamilton ordered.

Xiaoli watched the scanner for a moment. "Commander Sh'zaoqoq, please relax in a more comfortable position, legs straight and arms at your side."

The Arneci woman moved her legs, nearly gasping for strength. Xiaoli changed several settings on Thevoss's suit. The deep-blue shimmer brightened, and the suit became an abstract mirror laying before them.

"Time for what, Doctor?" asked Abol, now looking with deep concern to Thevoss's unmoving form.

Again, there was a pause from the ship. *"It's possible there is enough 'leakage', so to speak, to affect the fetus and its development. Any reverse time-flow effects might cause... miscarriage."*

"No..." Abol shook his head, almost violently.

"At ease, Commander," said Hamilton, laying a hand on his shoulder. "We'll do everything we can as quickly as we can." She looked to the hatch and the power-panel beside it. "Get that hatch opened and we'll do this. Doctor, prepare for our arrival within fifteen minutes. Hamilton out."

Abol stood, scanned the panel once again, and pressed several buttons on his PADD with trembling hands. Nothing happened. He reset the instrument, tried again.

Nothing. He swore in Arneci and turned away.

Hamilton stood and took him aside. "Look at me, Abol! We need you now! Your passion is real and understood, but right now we need the Chief Engineer. Stay with me. Do your duty."

"My bondmate is ill and our child dying! And you ask for duty!"

"Yes." Hamilton put her hands to Abol's shoulders and looked him in the eye. "Stay with me. We will find a way together. Trust."

"Commander!" Butler's shout drew Hamilton's attention. She looked to the hatch. It was slowly swinging open.

* * *

The station observed with fascination. Something was obviously wrong with one of the dark-skinned creatures, nearly collapsing against the pink-skinned one it had determined to be the leader. Communications flowed between the leader and the larger vessel, now very close to the station. Nearly too close. The station had not enough processing power available to decipher the information, and it would not likely have made any sense, considering the time-flow issues. Yet the creature now on the floor was in obvious distress.

Should the station allow them to leave, would they return? What if the station did not allow them passage to their small craft? Would they attempt to force the hatch? Their weapons likely didn't have enough power to burn through the hatch, but they could do considerable damage to the controls, and possibly force the lock.

Fascinating. The station had not considered such an event. Might it be a trick? The station's sensors could not penetrate the stasis fields, but optical scanners showed definite physical anxiety and changes in color. There were beads of… something emerging from within the affected creature's forehead. The optical interfaces on the front of the affected creature's head were dull and nearly unresponsive. Yes, this was no trick, and now the station had a decision to make. Release the creatures, with no certainty they would return, or keep them here, attending their fallen comrade.

The station considered. These creatures had shown care with their investigations. While their probing equipment had found many of the station's abilities, nothing critical or confidential had been breached. The trade of information gleaned from the larger vessel was certainly worth what small secrets the station had given up.

At the last, the station decided; it would allow the creatures their exit, if that was what they desired. The station understood the importance of life and keeping it fit. As one intelligent entity to another, it would certainly not deny the chance to live.

* * *

EAS Agincourt…

Hamilton contacted the captain, filling him in on events and advising him of her conversation with Dr. Kamisori as the shuttle entered the hangar deck.

"I had a similar one myself," said Westermann from the Bridge. *"We'll discuss later, but the priority is to get Commander Sh'zaoqoq to Sickbay. When she's stabilized and Chief Abol is with her, report to my ready room. We have other pressing issues."*

"Aye, sir. We're all glad to be back on board." Hamilton closed the contact and watched as Sh'zaoqoq was wheeled from the shuttle down the corridor to the turbolift. Abol followed, speaking quietly in Arneci to his bondmate, even though she was frozen in time with the stasis unit running.

Hamilton followed with the rest of the landing party, but there was no room for them in the lift car with the gurney. They waited as the doors closed, looking to one another. At last the First Officer's eyes stayed with Xiaoli's.

"Assessment, Commander? How intelligent is the station, and was releasing us a cognizant choice or just an automatic response of a safety protocol?"

The science officer pondered for moments as the others watched and waited. "If I were to assign odds, I would say perhaps seventy percent the AI was aware of Commander Sh'zaoqoq's distress." She almost showed a smile. "If I were to assign odds."

"Commander," said Butler, looking to each of the women, "you're saying the station is alive? AI, I can understand, but to recognize a medical issue of an alien species requires awareness of a high order. The ability to comprehend another being's pain or discomfort, and act in a manner to assist..." His voice trailed as he shook his head.

"Not necessarily," continued Xiaoli. "The station has obvious optical receptors, auditory receivers, and an enormous amount of computing power. In nearly every sentient species we have encountered, there are certain common traits regarding illness or pain. To observe one of us exhibiting behavior not seen, and the others of the party moving to assist, should be a simple problem to calculate and draw conclusion from."

"True sentience, though," replied Butler, "would mean life, wouldn't it? Feelings? Emotions?"

Xiaoli raised an eyebrow and traded glances with Hamilton, who only grinned and spoke. "Sounds like you have a pupil, Commander. Perhaps when this emergency is over, you can assist the Lieutenant in some of your experiments with AI's and their thought processes."

Butler began to speak, but the lift doors opened, and they crowded in together. "Sickbay," said Hamilton, pressing the intercom button. "We'll all see Commander Sh'zaoqoq is settled and Chief Abol is with her, then I need your reports in the next couple of hours. Technically, none of you are on ship's duty, but the captain is expecting our review to determine whether or not we're returning to the station."

"I hope he'll allow us to," said Xiaoli. "It's a fascinating artifact and deserves further study."

"I agree, Commander, but at the same time, we can't be sure what the continued exposure to the reverse time-flow might be. If it can affect Thevoss, there is no guarantee it won't show others harm… however unintentional."

The lift door opened. They hurried down the corridor to Sickbay. Hamilton followed more slowly, thinking of what else might be on the captain's mind, and wary of his last words.

* * *

Hamilton stopped by her quarters long enough for a quick sonic shower and a change of uniform after leaving Sickbay. She longed for a real shower, or maybe lounging in a hot tub, but the captain was waiting, and Earthfleet Long Range Explorers were not blessed with such niceties as hot tubs.

She entered the Bridge, nodded to the officers at their stations, and buzzed the ready room.

Westermann stood as she entered. "Welcome back, Commander." He motioned to the desk. "I ordered tea for us. Take a moment and tell me about your experiences."

Hamilton poured tea, sweetened it with honey, and

sipped, thinking. "Commander Sh'zaoqoq is out of stasis and stable. Dr. Kamisori says she'll be fine. Everyone in the party is terribly dehydrated and Sickbay had them all hooked up to IV's when I left. The environmental suits do that, you know."

Westermann nodded, watching his first officer carefully. "Give me a quick summary so we can decide how best to proceed. I've already gotten a call from Xiaoli, almost begging a chance to return to the station. I need your advice."

Hamilton stared into her cup. "Captain, we've never encountered anything like this. We have the run of a completely alien artifact with no interference at all to learn its secrets."

"Not exactly true, Lori. The station itself has shown the ability to test us. I can't believe that won't continue. At what point does it become seriously dangerous? How will the station know what's lethal and what's only a bump on the head?"

Hamilton considered. "No, sir, I can't believe that now. Even with my natural caution, as you've called it, I don't believe the station will purposely harm us. Test us, yes, because that's likely what it's programmed to do. Harm… I just don't see it, after what we went through."

"So your official recommendation is that we return?"

Hamilton paused, then grinned. "You realize we've switched places here? You're being cautious while I'm all gung-ho?" She laughed. After a moment, Westermann joined her.

"Very well, Commander. Who do you want to replace the Chief and his bondmate?"

"I'll take one of the younger E-Techs. It's a good exercise. Butler is proving to be a good foil for the science officer. I've suggested they work together after this mission is over."

Westermann nodded. "We have a couple of other issues to talk about. The first being Dr. Kamisori."

Hamilton sighed. "Yes, sir. I know you requested her for *Agincourt,* but she just doesn't seem to have the temperament for shipboard life. She actually snapped at Abol when we brought Thevoss into Sickbay. It's a concern, yes."

"The other issue is, where are the Qoearc? And if we're only a couple of light years from a Stiz outpost, should we be worrying about them as well?"

"Yet no sign of either, right?"

"Tactical and Sciences find no trace… yet. But for some reason, I can't shake the feeling we're not out of this. Someone will always show up to make it… interesting."

Hamilton pondered for a moment as she refilled their teacups. "*Agincourt* is a match for anything the Qoearc have, sir, as long as we're not blind and without countermeasures. As for the Stiz, their only advantage is their energy field system. Their ships aren't much more than assault shuttles with better weapons."

"And this star system isn't likely something they'd be interested in, except for the station itself. Regardless, we've got to stay alert." Westermann thought as he drained his cup. "Plan on returning to the station in twenty-four hours. That will give everyone time to rest and recuperate. No more than three days, Lori. We're pushing our luck here now. And you know the concerns from Dr. Kamisori's 'hobbyist' regarding what might happen to this station due to the time-flow difference."

"Aye, sir. We'll do what we can in three days, then wrap it up. But I would sure love to meet these people who built the station. They'd be worthy to consider for membership in the Earth Alliance."

* * *

The station watched the small craft depart the hangar. The other two, obviously positioned to see into the observation deck through the main viewports from space, left as well, one ahead, the other trailing. All three entered a large port at the lower rear of the main vessel, first the craft which held the incapacitated creature, then the others, hovering in protection. The hatches closed, and the station was again alone.

It proceeded to turn most of its power to the large vessel once more, but part of it calculated whether the creatures would return for further study. The percentage was better than half, it decided, and it went about devising other tests. Tests of logic and of reasoning power, tests of will or courage… all non-lethal, but more difficult than those before. It had to know more about these creatures, and if they were truly worthy of contact with the creators, regardless the time-flow difference.

One test became rather interesting, and it considered deeply of the implications. How would the large ship react, if the station could keep it close by, not allowing it to leave when it wished? Would those aboard react with weapons, or try to reason their way out? The station's first deduction said reason would be the initial attempt, but if the station persisted in holding the vessel close, hostilities could result.

The station knew it had no weapons or defenses to match that of the large vessel. It was obviously a ship of war, no matter how the creatures tried to hide it. It also knew the creators could not defeat it. After all, the creators were wise and benevolent, not a species that mounted weapons of destruction on their ships. Therefore, these creatures were much, much younger than those who built the station.

In the last assessment, the station decided to proceed with its testing, even if it chanced repercussions. It must know. It was programmed to know. It was a machine, but a very, very smart one. As smart as these creatures, surely. Perhaps even more so.

But now, there were other considerations, ones that might make all these suppositions meaningless. The station had turned its long-range scanners far beyond the system when certain alarms were tripped. There it detected signatures like those seen when the large vessel was first approaching. These others, unique and closing fast, would present new samples for evaluation.

The station began to think in terms of not only study and inquiry, but survival. And if survival wasn't possible, then final protocols and directives. It began to prepare a message to its creators. Humans might have thought the message as a last will and testament.

Four
Uninvited Guests

"Duty Log, Captain Noah Westermann, 030717.10. The landing party returned to the alien station two days ago and is currently involved in mapping critical circuitry and the sensor array. Commander Hamilton reports no further issues with the station testing them, and all hands are in good spirits. Science Officer Xiaoli has requested permission to contact the Earthfleet Academy and present our findings once we return to Fleet Base Twelve, but that decision will be up the chain of command. But sending a team of the best scientists in the Earth Alliance to further study this artifact would be a prudent decision.

"In the meantime, we have had no indication of Qoearc, Stiz, or anyone else in the vicinity. It appears my original fears of being followed were false."

* * *

EAS Agincourt…

"Captain, I'm picking up hyperlight signatures at the edge of the system border." Phillips, at Tactical, turned to the command chair. "Two… no, three… no, four!"

Westermann looked to Xiaoli's second, David Harvey, at Sciences. "What do we have, Lieutenant?"

"Confirmed, sir, four signatures have just appeared, three smaller, one larger. They appear to be Qoearc and have dropped out of hyperlight."

Westermann blew a breath and hit the intercom. "Sickbay, Bridge. Dr. Kamisori, is Commander Sh'zaoqoq fit for duty?"

A pause on the line as Westermann heard voices exchanging information. Finally, Kamisori spoke. *"She's fine, I released her yesterday and told her to take twenty-four hours off before returning to duty."*

Westermann counted to ten, then the lift doors opened. Sh'zaoqoq stepped onto the Bridge. "Permission to return to duty, Captain?"

He nodded, relieved to see her, but furious with Kamisori's report. "She's here now, Doctor. Next time you release one of my Bridge crew for duty, be sure to inform me."

"It's in my daily report." Kamisori broke the link. Westermann fumed. "Welcome back, Commander, please relieve the lieutenant. Mr. Phillips, assist Sciences at the auxiliary station. Tactical, Sciences, full report in five minutes."

He turned to the Comm station. "Get me Commander Hamilton, quickly. Engineering, full assessment of the ship, now."

"Hamilton here. What's going on, Captain?"

"Qoearc found our trail, Commander. Get everyone back on board *Agincourt* within," he looked to Sciences. Harvey held up five fingers. "Within five hours. As soon as they locate this station, they'll head in-system."

"Aye, sir. We're in the middle of some fascinating stuff, Captain. It may take us a bit longer to finish our upload of information."

"You've tapped into their computer?"

"Not exactly, but we have access to some records that don't appear to be encrypted. For all we know, it could be the lunch menu."

"Take no chances, Commander. That's an order." He heard Hamilton sigh.

"Yes, sir. Five hours max. We'll wrap it up as soon as possible. Landing party out."

Westermann clicked off, peered at the screens, one showing the station, the other a feed from one of the assault shuttles watching through the station ports. He looked around the Bridge, all hands busy at their stations. "Tactical?"

"Four Qoearc confirmed, sir. Three *Tak'nar* scouts, the other possibly as large as a *Cotak* cruiser."

"But not *Vrex* class?"

Sh'zaoqoq ran her fingers over the buttons quickly, enhancing, sharpening, refining the readings. She turned. "Confirmed, sir. *Vrex*."

The Bridge was quiet for a long moment.

Westermann looked to Engineering. "Status?"

"Green board, sir. Full sublight, thrusters, and hyperlight power. All PAKS weapons are operational, we have a full load of torpedoes, and the accumulators are charged to maximum. One assault shuttle on the deck and ready to launch, the other two are standing off the station."

"Captain." Harvey's voice from Sciences drew Westermann's attention. "Minimum time to our location by the Qoearc is about seven hours. That's if they push it hard. At cruising speed, which they'll probably do at least in the beginning, we estimate nine to ten hours. Doubtful they'll find the station at all until they get closer to the planet."

Westermann nodded. "Keep an eye on them, gentlemen. He looked to Sh'zaoqoq. "Commander, is the Chief back in Engineering?"

The Arneci woman smiled briefly. Yes, sir, and much relieved. Thank you for taking care of me."

"That was…" Westermann paused. "The good doctor's doing, not mine. Regardless, we're all glad to see you well."

The Bridge grew quiet again, this time with duties and a feeling of growing anticipation.

* * *

The Station…

Hamilton made her rounds, checking with each of the landing party as they finalized their work. She had set the two security guards packing equipment not being used, transferring it to the shuttle, and offered words of encouragement to Xiaoli, Butler, and the others as she could, working hard to glean as much data as they could from the station's memory banks.

In time, she called a halt. As the last equipment was shut down, and as she made her final check, her intercom buzzed.

"Commander Hamilton, Agincourt. This is an OC transmission!"

She stopped short of the hatch and pressed the button. "Go ahead, *Agincourt*."

"Westermann. Lori, we've got two Qoearc Tak'nar scouts that just appeared on our screens, not ten minutes away. Tactical is trying to figure out how they got here so fast, but it doesn't matter. We're in trouble."

"Understood. We're packing now, we'll leave what we don't need and return to *Agincourt* immediately."

"No time. You'll have to shelter somewhere in the station or the shuttle. Your escorts will attempt to draw the Tak'nars away from the station. Keep your eyes peeled for an opening, but do not risk your life and crew. Understood?"

"Sir, there's no place on this station that's safe. The hull is no better than an assault shuttle hull, and we find no evidence of weapons or defenses other than for micro-meteorites. This thing is a tin can."

"Then it's the shuttle. At least you have countermeasures, and if you don't disembark, they may not even detect you. Again, keep alert and watch for a strategic opening to return to Agincourt."

Hamilton's thoughts spun. "Yes, sir. We'll do what we can. Hamilton out." She clicked off and stuck her head through the hatchway. "All hands, into the shuttle on the double. We're under attack!"

* * *

EAS Agincourt...

"Commander Sh'zaoqoq, explain to me what the hell happened?

"Captain, I have no idea. The *Tak'nar* scouts went stealth and we lost track of them. The third stayed with the battlecruiser, and they're still three hours away at maximum speed."

"Why didn't you tell me about the *Tak'nars*?"

Sh'zaoqoq turned slowly to Westermann. "Sir, I thought I did. You acknowledged... did you not?"

Westermann's eyes stayed locked with hers for a long moment. "Weapons status?"

She returned to her panel. "Fully powered. Shall we go to Battle Stations?"

Westermann opened his mouth to speak, then closed it. "I ordered Battle Stations when the *Tak'nars* were first detected." He looked to Phillips and Harvey, standing together at the Science station. "Didn't I?"

"I... might not have heard, sir. I was engaged in..." Phillips straightened. "No, sir, I heard no such order. Sorry."

"The time-flow effects are mounting," said Harvey, his

face nearly tucked into a hooded scanner. "And the station has extended it to within five kilometers of *Agincourt*. The field is growing in intensity also, glowing in the ultraviolet range. Much stronger and it will get into the visible frequencies."

"Sir," continued Harvey, now standing, "without stasis gear, we're fully exposed to whatever effects the reverse time-flow might have on us. Obviously more serious than what the landing party is getting."

Westermann hit the intercom. "Sickbay, Bridge. I'm sending Commander Sh'zaoqoq back to you. Put her in immediate medical stasis. She'll explain when she arrives."

"Captain, this is Dr. Kamisori. There is no need for theatrics. We understand the problem."

"Then why…" Westermann held his temper, but only barely. "Follow my orders, Doctor. Bridge out." He looked to Sh'zaoqoq. "Sickbay, Commander."

"Sir, please allow me to do my duty."

"Your duty right now is to yourself and your unborn. Get to Sickbay. Ensign, escort the Commander."

Sh'zaoqoq rose and walked slowly to the lift with the security officer, not looking at the Bridge crew. Phillips quietly took her seat.

"Update, Mr. Phillips. Where are the Qoearc?"

The lieutenant ran his fingers over the controls. "Five minutes out and drifting closer. They've surely spotted us by now, but they're very wary. Basically, they're hanging in space, just out of range."

"Shuttle and the escorts?"

Phillips from Sciences answered. "The shuttle is fully loaded, all hands accounted for. The escorts have turned and are facing the Qoearc. Our weapons are charged and ready."

Westermann blew a breath. *At least someone knows what to do,* he thought. *Between the time-flow effects and Dr. Kamisori's near-insubordination…*

* * *

The station watched the changing events with growing interest. The two newly-arrived ships seemed to pop out of nowhere, and were of different design and construction. They had taken an aggressive posture against the two small ships watching the station. When those ships swung around, the station noted immediate changes in the energy state of the new ships. Obviously, weapons being charged, and some sort of energy field surrounded them, likely for defense.

The station was fascinated. It had not anticipated this, and now it had two species to study; two species who apparently knew each other well and were adversaries. Why so?

The station filed the question and turned its attention to the creatures still within it. They had boarded their small craft, but not disembarked. Likely because they would be attacked, was the reasoning. And gauging the energy output of the new ships, destruction would be an almost-certainty.

The station extended its time-flow barrier, more for its own protection than anything else, and brought additional resources online. It knew this could be detected easily by the crew on board, and likely the other ships as well, but it could not be helped. The station must protect itself, however it could. But its capabilities were limited. The creators had not thought of hostilities in this space, and therefore, not prepared for it.

The station initiated its secondary processors for analysis. It calculated probabilities, estimated flight times between the craft within its hangar and the ship from which it came. It determined by observation and analyzing energy readings the large ship could quite easily defeat the two smaller new arrivals, if it had similar capabilities. It crunched numbers, evaluated strategies, projected outcomes. It also was completely aware of the other two ships quickly approaching, one nearly as large as the original close by. Should they arrive before the two new ones were defeated, the original large vessel likely would not survive.

The station reviewed its options, which were few. While it had no concept of friend or foe, it knew those who had been aboard were curious creatures, as were the creators, and had taken steps to investigate with care.

The station was not so certain of those who had just arrived.

* * *

Westermann ordered environmental suits with stasis fields for the Bridge crew and auxiliary control once it was confirmed the station had expanded its time-flow field. The order was passed down to Engineering, the torpedo deck, PAKS control, and other critical systems. When the supply of suits was exhausted, Chief Abol recommended portable stasis units be assembled around whatever else was necessary, including Sickbay. Dr. Kamisori had her own thoughts about the idea.

"We don't need it, Captain. Sickbay has standard shielding plus the environmental barrier, as you know. This intrusion is unnecessary."

"Your point is taken, Doctor, but my orders stand. Sickbay will have a portable stasis unit in place and operating within half an hour. It is not to be tampered with. No argument."

"This will go into my report."

Westermann laughed. "I certainly hope so. Your personal opinion carries no weight where the safety of crew and ship are concerned. As long as this time-flow issue is present, I'll do whatever is necessary to protect

Agincourt. You said it yourself, it's affecting us. End of discussion." He clicked off. "Sciences, report."

Harvey turned from his panel. "Captain, the Qoearc *Tak'nars* haven't moved for thirty minutes. My assessment is, they are waiting for arrival of the other ships."

"Agreed. We have what, a bit more than two hours? Tactical, I need a plan to get the shuttle and its escorts back to *Agincourt* safely. Get me something quickly." Westermann hit the intercom switch again. "Commander Hamilton, report."

Lori Hamilton's voice was worn but she responded quickly. *"Nominal, Captain. Everyone is worried, but there's little we can do at this time."*

"We're working on it. I'll have a plan within fifteen minutes. We've got to get everyone on board and clear orbit before the other Qoearc arrive. Stay in touch, and if anything changes on the station, advise me immediately."

"Aye, sir. Hamilton out."

Westermann clicked off again. "Engineering, what sort of cover could we provide for the shuttles? Plasma ejection, debris field, anything. Defensive drones? Coordinate with Tactical and get me an answer." He turned once more to Sciences. Harvey's face was in his scanning viewer again. "What is it, Lieutenant?"

"Sir…" Harvey's voice trailed as he adjusted his controls. "Something at the edge of the system, but I'm not sure what. Possibly more ships."

"How many?"

"Two only, sir, and they're pretty small, barely detectable. At first I thought they were just noise."

Westermann faced Phillips at Tactical again. "Talk to me."

The lieutenant's hands ran over his panel quickly and scanned readouts. "Confirmed, sir, two small ships, heading in-system now at high speed. ETA, three hours, maybe less. They're really moving."

Harvey motioned for attention. "Sir, thermal scans show heat content in the ships over two hundred Celsius."

Westermann blinked and looked to Tactical. "Stiz. Not what we need right now, but they might be our saviors." Mister Phillips, track them as they approach. I need to know if they are on the same course as the approaching Qoearc and if they can overtake them. I need it now."

"Sir." Phillips turned once more to his panel.

Westermann pressed the intercom button. "Commander Hamilton, *Agincourt*. Lori, we've got more company. The Stiz have decided to join the party and they're coming in..." he looked to Phillips at Tactical, giving a nod and thumbs-up. "Tracking the approaching Qoearc. Tactical says they'll all arrive about the same time." Phillips nodded to Westermann again. "So we're out of options. You're going to have to make a run for it."

The line was quiet, but he could hear voices talking over options and debating. Finally, Hamilton replied. *"Understood sir. Just tell us what we need to do, and we'll follow orders as best we can. I'm assuming the assault shuttles will provide cover."*

Westermann began to answer, then paused. "What if they didn't? What if you simply left the station and headed for *Agincourt*?"

Hamilton was silent as she considered. *"Suggestion. Advise the Qoearc we're here and are now returning to the ship. After that, we'll leave the vicinity peacefully."*

"And then?"

"No idea, sir, but if it works, at least we're in one piece and

back on board."

Westermann thought it over. "I'll contact them immediately, but since we've had no messages from either ship, my guess is they won't acknowledge. At the same time, with Stiz in the neighborhood, they may well want to leave while they can as well." He let go a breath. "Okay, we'll try it. Stay put. I'll get back to you." He clicked off and turned to the Comm station. "Get me the Qoearc. Whichever one won't hang up on you."

* * *

The Station…

Hamilton huddled with her landing party, discussing options, strategies, and talking with the assault shuttles regarding withdrawal options. Commander Xiaoli offered to pilot, saying her quick reflexes would be a good match for the Qoearc's tactics in similar situations.

"You've studied Qoearc tactics?" asked Hamilton. "You continue to astound me, Commander. Very well, prepare to disembark on the captain's order, but not before. The rest of you, be sure you're strapped in tightly, it may be bumpy. And it might be best if we all went into medical stasis just in case."

The crew traded glances. Butler nodded and spoke. "What if… we launched the shuttle empty?"

Hamilton shook her head after a moment. "For what purpose, Lieutenant?"

"To see if they'd shoot it down, Commander. I'd rather take that chance with us not in it."

"Damn, that's brilliant," said one of the S-Techs.

"We can always have one of the other shuttles take us on either way," continued Butler.

"Yes, and if they shoot down the assault shuttles, we're stranded," said Hamilton.

"We can cross individually in our suits," replied Xiaoli. "It would be a lengthy and somewhat unnerving transit, but possible."

"Unnerving?" Hamilton showed a slight smile. "Damn scary, Commander. Look, we could debate this at length. For the moment, unless ordered otherwise, we stay with the shuttle." She looked to Butler. "But I'll pass along the suggestion to the captain."

* * *

The station watched closely as the new arrivals approached. All of them. The two latest were of a uniqueness never seen. Some sort of organic structure in the vessel's hull! The occupants were not of carbon base, but silicon! How incredible!

Quick calculations were made to show that very soon, the space around the station would be occupied by three different species, all apparently at odds with each other for unknown reasons. Results of combat between them would likely be disastrous for all involved, including the station itself. There was little choice, therefore, and the station began preparations. It would take the majority of power available, but it must be done, for any hope of survival. For anyone.

* * *

EAS Agincourt…

"Captain, the station field is expanding again!" Harvey's voice from Science interrupted Westermann's focus on the forward screens. "Visible spectrum, deep blue, energy output has nearly tripled! Getting way too close, sir!"

"At ease, Lieutenant, just give me the facts. Tactical, what are the Qoearc doing?"

"Backing away quickly, sir. We might have an opening to send the shuttle across in about three minutes. The field is within a kilometer of *Agincourt*."

"ETA on the other Qoearc and Stiz?"

Phillips ran his fingers over the panel controls. "Ten minutes for both, give or take two. The Stiz acceleration has been—"

"Never mind that, thank you." Westermann turned to Skovok at the Comm station. "Reply from the Qoearc?"

"None, sir. I've hailed both ships three times."

"Raise Commander Hamilton." He waited as he watched the screens. The Qoearc were definitely retreating, but keeping weapons trained on the station and the assault shuttles.

"Commander Hamilton, sir." Skovok adjusted his earpiece. "The connection is very bad. The time-flow effects are interfering."

Westermann punched his intercom button. "Lori, we may have our chance coming up. You're going to have to watch carefully from your perspective and decide what's best and when. If you deem it safer to remain in the station hangar, do so. At this point the Qoearc are as worried as we are and retreating." He waited for a reply, but heard only static on the line. "Commander Hamilton, are you there?"

"Here, sir..." Hamilton's voice faded. *"...didn't hear everything... said. Keeping an... on the Qoearc...effects are... headaches and dizzy, don't... know if we can pilot the shuttle."*

"Hold on, Commander. Mr. Harvey, condition of the assault shuttle crews?"

Again, Harvey peered into the scanner and made controls adjustments. "Sir, they've not reported anything serious, but they have better shielding than the shuttle on the station. Shall I have them pull back?"

"Tell them to take position around the hangar where Commander Hamilton's shuttle will emerge. They are to escort the landing party back to *Agincourt* as quickly as possible."

"Aye, sir." Harvey turned to Skovok at the Comm station and gave quiet orders.

"Lori, listen carefully. The assault shuttles will meet you at the hangar entrance. They will run cover for you. Tell your pilot to make a beeline for *Agincourt's* main hangar deck. Get in quickly, don't worry about damage to the shuttle. Just get where you're protected from the time-flow effects. Confirm, Commander."

Again, static met Westermann's ears for a tense moment. *"…hear you… okay, got it, I think… not fun… take off in two… acknowledge, please."*

"Tactical, two minutes. Get those assault shuttles in place now." Westermann turned to his intercom again. "Acknowledged, Commander, we'll get you home safe. Keep this line open." He turned. "Mr. Phillips, target PAKS port and starboard on those two Qoearc. If they so much as twitch, hit them hard."

"Captain, the Qoearc are five minutes away, Stiz six, seven at most."

"Damn! Commander, get out of there. Qoearc are coming down our throats with the Stiz in hot pursuit. Go now!"

"Aye… launch… away and clear…"

"Tactical, launch the third assault shuttle for additional cover. Helm, swing us around, bow-on to the Qoearc. I want them to understand what will happen if they fire."

"Captain, we're getting aberrant readings in sensors, targeting computers." Phillips quickly ran a diagnostic. "Likely the time-flow effects, sir."

"Confirmed," said Harvey. "Our sensor net is slowly degrading. We've got about ten minutes before we're basically blind."

Flashes of thought recalling the pulsar event ran through Westermann's mind. He almost chuckled at the irony. "Engineering, can we shield our computer core any further?"

"Sir, we have a full-size planetary habitation unit running at max power. We're out of options."

"Captain, the shuttle is about five minutes to docking. It won't make it to *Agincourt* before the Qoearc and Stiz arrive."

"They're here!" Phillips at Tactical nearly leapt from his chair.

Decelerating hard, the incoming Qoearc ships appeared as if from nowhere. The battlecruiser loomed huge, a thousand meters behind the *Tak'nar* scouts. A minute later, two Stiz ships arrived, much less imposing, but Westermann knew they carried a lethal weapon in their energy cocoon. He also knew it took at least two Stiz ships to generate it. A tactical mistake, in his mind, for the Stiz to send only two against the forces gathered.

"Shuttle time to *Agincourt*?" Westermann looked to Harvey at Sciences.

"Three minutes, sir. The field continues to intensify. Five hundred meters and closing. In five minutes, we'll be within it."

"Noted. Commander Hamilton, your status?" Static again, and nothing else. "Lori, respond."

Phillips glanced over his shoulder. "Captain, the shuttle is starting to drift. Engines off, navigation out, other systems failing."

"Engineering, activate a grappler."

"Sir, the system is down and has been since we reported malfunctions earlier."

Westermann shook his head. "There was no such report..." He bit his tongue. He knew either the reports hadn't been made or he simply hadn't heard them because of the station's field effects. He knew a decision was coming... one he really didn't want to make.

* * *

The Shuttle...

Hamilton's head spun. She was on her stomach in the shuttle and had no idea how she had gotten there. She knew what she needed to do, she simply couldn't get her mind and voice to coordinate giving simple orders. Butler, beside her, was no better. The Techs were comatose. Xiaoli at the controls sat stoic, eyes closed, lips slightly parted, obviously in some sort of Zen state. Or dead.

Hamilton crawled to the control panel and hit the intercom switch on the third try. She knew she had heard the captain's voice, but didn't know if it was moments or hours ago.

The shuttle jolted and she fell. Another jolt, and beyond the viewport she could dimly see the assault shuttles nudging hers. They must have been drifting, for *Agincourt* hung in the distance, at least a kilometer away, and the assault shuttles were pushing them back on course. Hard to tell, with her eyes nearly crossed. A sharper jolt, and somewhere in her addled mind she knew one of the shuttles had engaged a tow line.

The hatch blew, and for an instant everything and everyone was sucked toward it. Then the air curtain engaged, the whirlwind stopped, and in stepped three suited figures. *Agincourt* security. Hamilton tried to grin, but only drooled down her chin inside her environmental suit.

One of the guards approached, said something, but she couldn't reply. She dimly felt herself being slung over his shoulder and hurried out, the guard linking to a line between the two craft. She was dropped onto the deck of the assault shuttle, none too gently, but barely felt the shock. She lay half-awake as voices filled with urgency ran between the hatchways. She knew she was safe, at least temporarily, and the captain had performed a miracle.

Not the first time, she thought. It was the clearest thought she'd had for what seemed a hundred years.

* * *

EAS Agincourt…

"All hands safe," reported Harvey. He turned to Westermann, grinning. "Well done, sir. Great idea."

"The credit goes to the assault shuttle crew, Lieutenant. Tactical, status."

"Qoearc have retreated to fifty kilometers relative, Captain. All but one scout, drifting slowly, perpendicular to our position and the station. Stiz are holding about one hundred kilometers behind the Qoearc line. They all seem to be out of the time-flow field effects."

"Mr. Harvey, how much time—"

"Captain! The scout is powering weapons! Firing!"

The drifting *Tak'nar* cut loose a barrage of fire in the general direction of the station. Most of the blasts missed.

A few struck the station causing visible damage and outgassing. As the *Tak'nar* continued to drift, its fire found the shuttles, cutting crooked paths across their hulls and engines.

"Damn it! Tactical, disable that ship, don't destroy it unless you have to. Battle Stations. Que lighting." Westermann hit the intercom as deep crimson lights bathed the Bridge. "Shuttles, do not return fire! Get back to *Agincourt*!"

With his targeting computers offline and scanners nearly blinded, Phillips used a steady eye and a bit of luck as he fired at the *Tak'nar*, cutting away one turret and sending the ship spinning away. His hand hovered near the controls as he watched for further weapons discharge, but the ship only slid further from the engagement, rotating slowly.

"Good work, Lieutenant. Status of the other Qoearc?"

Phillips shook his head, as if to clear it. "Sir… I think they're charging weapons, but it's hard to tell. I'm a bit dizzy."

"Captain, the rescue shuttle sustained engine damage and is drifting away. The others are following."

Westermann punched the intercom again. "Sickbay, Bridge. Get someone up here on the double with whatever you have to counteract the time-flow effects. I've got officers in trouble and I need them fully alert." He clicked off. "Mr. Harvey, assist at Tactical until Medical arrives." He turned to the Comm station again. "Get me the shuttle with the landing party."

* * *

Damage! The station immediately assessed what functions had been incapacitated by the energy blasts from the vessel still within the time-flow field. It was obvious whatever protection or shielding it had was not as effective as the beings who had been on the station carried.

It surmised the attack was an attempt to eliminate what it thought was causing the effects. Therefore, these creatures were much quicker to resort to hostilities than the first group.

The station instituted self-repairing systems, brought nanobots online, initiated fire-suppression, created shielding around damaged areas to keep smoke and particulate matter from dispersing, then powered up the remaining generators. It extended the time-flow barrier to its fullest. It knew this would encompass the larger vessel from which the creatures had come, but it could not be helped. The station must protect itself. It felt no remorse. Its programming in this regard was hardwired. There were no choices.

It watched as the small craft struggled for control and edged their way toward the parent ship. The space around the station and the vessels began to glow, well into the visible range beyond ultraviolet. Intensity grew. Pressures within the small craft mounted. The station calculated only moments remained before they were incapacitated completely.

* * *

Assault Shuttle One…

The hypo-spray through the medi-tap in the neck of Hamilton's suit hissed and was drawn away. Her mind cleared somewhat, and she rolled to her hands and knees. She worked her mouth slowly, more to see if she was injured than anything else.

"Report," she rasped. She took a deep breath, looking round. The rest of the landing party lay beside her in various stages of distress. Butler was sitting up, still glassy-eyed. The Techs were groaning but moving. Xiaoli was motionless on the deck, but breathing.

"She's in some sort of meditative state," said the security ensign. "But we're in trouble, Commander. Engines are out, life support on batteries, and the other ships aren't much better. But we've got to transfer to another shuttle."

"Get ready to move, then," replied Hamilton. "We'll cross in suits to save time. We've got to get out of this time effect. If we wait much longer, even *Agincourt* may not be able to get away."

"What about the Qoearc and Stiz?"

Hamilton shook her head. She stopped immediately, still dazed. "Doesn't matter. Alert the closest shuttle we're on our way." She looked to Butler. "Lieutenant, you and the Techs take Xiaoli, security will lead, I'll follow."

"Commander, permission to remain with you," said Butler.

She nodded after a moment. "Everyone else prepare to disembark."

The shuttle lurched, then alarms rang. A muffled explosion came from behind the rear bulkhead. Two seconds later, the wall exploded inward.

Two security men went down, and a Tech followed. Butler threw himself over Hamilton, catching the brunt of the explosion on his back. Debris ricocheted from wall to wall, crashing into the control panel, impaling the pilot, sending the shuttle spinning away from the others.

Hamilton rolled from beneath Butler. His suit was shredded from shoulders to waist. His helmet was fractured. And he was dead, a jagged piece of durasteel imbedded in his back.

The two remaining Techs dragged her away. "Commander, we've got to go. The hull is breached, and in a minute, we'll get blown out by the rupture."

"Get Xiaoli. Hit the vent button. Go." She pointed to the emergency vent controls beside the hatch.

The Techs gathered up the limp form of the science officer. One held her as the other worked the controls. The atmosphere screamed away through the emergency system ventilators. The hatch opened and the Techs stepped out with Xiaoli between them. They looked back, but only briefly.

Hamilton rose, or tried to. She looked at her left leg; blood streamed down and was now beginning to boil in the vacuum. *Didn't even feel it. Ooohhh, now I do!*

She stifled a scream, cracked open a patch packet and slapped it across the worst of the wound. Another followed. Then another. Her leg was numb, and the stim-shot wearing off. She crawled on hands and knees to the hatch.

She took the hatchway jamb in one hand and gave a quick look at the gash in her suit. It appeared to be holding.

She looked once more at the bodies, eyes spinning, head feeling as though filled with cotton. She convinced herself no one remained alive.

She braced against the torn framework and rose on one leg to push herself out the hatch…

… just as the shuttle exploded.

* * *

EAS Agincourt…

Med-Techs streamed onto the Bridge from the lift. Two went to Westermann, two more to Tactical, and others dispersed to every station. Each crew member was given a stim-shot, the captain two, and they laid Phillips on the deck to administer CPR. Three relief crew entered a moment later, one taking the Tactical chair, one the Aux. Services panel, and the other beside Westermann, awaiting orders.

The Med-Techs placed Phillips on a stretcher and carried him from the Bridge. Not a word had been spoken. Westermann assumed it was because they were in as bad of shape as everyone else.

He glanced around the Bridge. Most of the screens were dark. The Tactical panel was half-dead. Science Station instruments were blinking on and off. Harvey cursed to himself as he peered into his scanner. Skovok at Comm was engrossed in listening for any scrap of information from the shuttles. Engineering was balancing power to wherever it was needed most as best they could, the E-Techs speaking quietly together as they monitored every need.

"Tactical, report." Westermann's voice echoed in his ears. He swallowed and repeated the command.

"Sir… three shuttles, one slipping away slowly. That's got to be the one from the station. Two more are about three minutes from the hangar."

"Three… not four?"

The ensign checked his instruments again. "No, sir, only three. And what appears to be a spreading debris field behind them."

Westermann turned to Skovok. "Get me Commander Hamilton, whatever it takes."

Skovok nodded, listening to his headset, then held a hand. He shook his head. "Captain, no reply. And I have a faint signal from shuttle two. They're approaching the hangar deck with casualties."

"Captain, there are several transponders I can't track," reported Harvey. He turned. "One is Commander

Hamilton's."

"Get me the shuttle."

Skovok paused, then looked to Westermann. "Audio only, sir."

"Shuttle, Bridge. What's going on?"

"Entering the hangar deck now, sir, two shuttles returning. The station shuttle was lost. The third of our group was destroyed. We have casualties and took losses. Including… Commander Hamilton."

Westermann seethed, and knew it was in part the two stim-shots. He swore silently at Dr. Kamisori and her ministrations. "Are you certain? Did you attempt rescue?"

A long pause as voices conferred over the comm. A new voice spoke. *"Sir, this is S-Tech Martina Lopez. The Commander ordered us to abandon the shuttle. She was to follow. Before she could exit, the shuttle exploded. We lost Lieutenant Butler and several others, as well."* A sob. *"I'm sorry."*

The Bridge was silent. Westermann's eyes stung and his heart raced. He looked at the port screen, flickering back to life, and the station in the distance. "Put the pilot on, Ensign."

Another pause. *"Yes, sir?"*

"All shuttles and survivors on board?"

"Aye, sir, and the hangar deck is secured."

Westermann clicked off. "Helm, ease us out of this… effect. Very carefully. Course 180, mark 0. Just back us away, thrusters only."

"Aye, sir. Helm is sluggish, but answering."

Agincourt moved slowly from the time-flow effect. Westermann watched as the view changed to the Qoearc in the distance.

"Captain, the undamaged *Tak'nars* have taken the third

one in tow. All Qoearc ships are powering engines. Looks like they're preparing to leave." The ensign whose name Westermann couldn't recall reported from Tactical. He could only nod in reply.

His head slowly began to clear. Hamilton... gone. Butler. Others of the landing party dead or injured. The shuttle crew. He looked at the station on the screen once again, fighting urges he knew were wrong.

"Captain, the Qoearc are moving off," said Harvey at Sciences. "I scanned life-signs before they headed out. They have massive casualties and serious damage to their systems. They were in no shape to fight, if it had come to that."

Westermann drew a breath. "Fortunate for all of us it didn't." He stared at the station on the screen, still debating his feelings.

"Captain, the Stiz ships are moving in."

It took a moment for the report to register. "Moving in where? Toward *Agincourt*?"

"No, sir, toward the station."

Westermann watched, fascinated. The Stiz ships took position near the station, well within the time-flow effect. A cloud of... something, plasma, chemicals, he simply wasn't sure, emanated from both ships, but each a different color and consistency.

"Captain, I'm getting readings... well, they simply don't register except as 'insufficient data'." Harvey at Sciences glanced at the screen, then back to his board.

"What the hell..."

"At easy, Mr. Phillips. Report."

"The... cloud is beginning to coalesce. The... ah, ships are..."

Westermann nodded agreement, entranced. "Mr. Skovok, get this on vid recording!"

"Already doing so, sir. And backup."

The bridge was nearly silent, watching as the Stiz ships literally began to dissolve.

"Not complete dissolution," said Harvey from Sciences. "Sir, it's like they're… blowing a bubble."

"Energy spiking, Captain!" Phillips nearly shouted from the Tactical board. Off the charts!"

"Get me an estimate on completion, quickly." Westermann turned to the E-Tech. "Status. Power, propulsion, everything."

"Sir, sublight is at fifty percent, hyperlight power not yet back online. Chief Abol reports they're running diagnostics and do not recommend any maneuvers."

"Weapons status, Tactical?"

"Captain, PAKS batteries are at forty percent, torpedo launchers are still offline. Countermeasures are at sixty percent, but that's wavering a bit."

"Comm, get the Stiz online."

Skovok worked at his panel for a moment. "No reply, sir."

"Do you have their frequency? Can we send, regardless if they're listening?"

"Yes, sir. We can loop a message into their system."

Westermann nodded. "Good. Put me through." He waited until Skovok nodded once more. "Attention Stiz vessels. This is Captain Noah Westermann commanding *EAS Agincourt*. Stand down. Leave this vicinity peacefully. This station…" he paused, considering what he was about to say. "This station and the planet it orbits are under the protection of Earthfleet and Earth Alliance. Any attack on the station or planet will be considered an act of war. This is your only warning. Stand down and leave this system." He motioned Skovok to leave the line open.

The lift doors opened and Thevoss Sh'zaoqoq took two steps onto the Bridge. "Permission to resume my duties, Captain?"

Westermann watched her closely. She was pale, or was that just the lighting? "You've been released by Dr. Kamisori?"

"Yes, sir. I am fit for duty." She waited, looking first at Westermann, then the screen, showing the Stiz, enveloping the station with their energy field.

"Welcome back, Commander. Take your place at Tactical and the ensign will assist you as needed."

"Thank you, sir." She crossed slowly, as the ensign offered the chair.

"Full report, Commander. Sciences, strength of the Stiz hulls and any defenses."

Sh'zaoqoq scanned her instruments as the ensign updated her. "Completion within fifteen minutes, sir. No apparent defensive energy screens, weapons, or countermeasures. Hull…" she looked over her shoulder to Harvey at Sciences.

"Similar to tritainium, Captain, but not quite as dense."

Westermann watched the screen, still flickering, but improving in clarity. "Commander Sh'zaoqoq, can you pierce that bubble with our particlebeams?"

Again, she ran her fingers over the controls. "Yes, sir, but that would only deter them for a while, most likely. Stiz are notoriously persistent in their attacks."

"Supposition or experience?" Westermann gave her a quick grin. "Alright, let's try a combination of things, then.

Pop that bubble. Let's see what they do."

Sh'zaoqoq and the ensign worked together to plot targeting solutions as the tactical computers came back online. They ran quick simulations. The Stiz construct was not stationary; it slowly expanded, then contracted toward the station as it solidified. With each passing moment it grew nearer to the station. The ships themselves seemed a part of the bubble.

After a moment, Sh'zaoqoq turned to Westermann. "Prepared, sir."

He nodded. "Fire when ready. Commander. Break that thing into a million pieces."

* * *

The station watched as the two intruders constructed what it analyzed as a particle-based energy field. The whole of the "bubble" for lack of a better term, was nearly solid light. The station had never seen anything like this, and wondered at first of the purpose. That soon became apparent, however. Further analysis confirmed, once the bubble was complete and drawn tightly about the station, it would begin draining away power, until nothing was left. This could not be allowed. But what could the station do?

It's time-flow system was operating at maximum, and apparently having no effect on the two bubble-building ships. The other vessel had moved away, beyond the now-visible glow of the station's time-flow effect, to safety. Therefore, the station did not have to consider that as part of its options.

But the station had no further defenses. It had no weapons. It calculated the energy required to short-circuit the bubble was just within its capability, but even that could only be done once, twice at most. And that action would not preclude the bubble-ships repeating their attack. For that is what the station now considered their actions as; an attack.

The only option left was a complete shutdown of all systems. Even the auto-startup could not be left running, for that would eventually be drained. And since it took power from the main source, in a trickle-effect, the outcome would be the same, however long it took. In fact, the bubble's energy-draining ability might be enough to crack the auto-start system and drain main power even more quickly.

But the station concluded even that wasn't enough. It could not conduct a full shutdown before the web was complete, not even under emergency conditions.

The station had no options. It could only watch and wait.

* * *

PAKS fire arced out from *Agincourt*, shattering the Stiz bubble. The Stiz ships reformed immediately, golden streamers of energy sparking in the time-flow glow.

Westermann watched as the Stiz ships stabilized themselves, then began to expand another bubble.

"Commander, this time I want you to catch the bubble dead center between the ships, then follow whatever traces are left right back up into the Stiz ships. Maybe we can damage their emitters."

Sh'zaoqoq recalibrated, adjusted, and aimed again. The ensign called off range and position softly as she made ready, then looked to Westermann. He nodded.

Again, the blue tracers struck the bubble. This time the PAKS tracers followed the sparkling streamers back to the Stiz ships. One cut the threads away, the other was too slow responding. Explosions rocked the ship, golden arcs of energy emitting from the everywhere. The ship began to drift, spinning slowly away. The other turned to face *Agincourt*.

"Stiz charging weapons, Captain," reported Sh'zaoqoq,

her hands steady on the firing controls.

"Let him make the first move, Commander. Comm, is our message still playing in their system?"

Skovok checked his instruments. "They've cut it off, sir. Likely several minutes ago."

"Very well. Polarization to the hull?" Westermann looked to Engineering.

"Seventy-five percent, sir, and steady."

"Tactical, prepare a light barrage if the Stiz fire. Warning shots. If they fire again, hit them hard."

"Aye, sir. Stiz are preparing to fire."

"Particlebeam incoming!"

Agincourt shook heavily with the impact. "Tactical, return fire, five seconds, half-power."

Sh'zaoqoq hit the buttons. Nothing happened.

"Fire control is down!" shouted the E-Tech.

"Helm, evasive, get us out of here!" Westermann hung on to the arms of his command chair as *Agincourt* pulled away on sublight power. "Engineering, get fire control up, now." He punched the intercom button. "Auxiliary control, who's in charge down there?"

A familiar voice came over the speaker. *"Xiaoli, Captain. We have very little working. Fire control is out here as well. Only one Stiz is pursuing, however."*

Agincourt shook again.

"They're on our tail, Captain. Hull polarization at forty-five percent!"

"Torpedoes?"

"Launchers… online, bow only!"

"Helm, bring us about, course 180 mark 0. Spin us around." Tactical, full spread."

Agincourt shuddered with the sudden course change.

"Helm is sluggish, but responding," reported Maddani.

"Nav is spotty, sir."

"Torpedoes armed and ready, Captain."

"Put one across their bow. Give them a warning shot."

Sh'zaoqoq fired. "Away."

The torpedo blossomed a hundred meters in front of the Stiz ship. It broke off immediately, turning back to the station.

"Stay on him, Helm. Tactical, if he opens fire on the station, take him out."

The Stiz slowed and stopped beside its drifting counterpart. Westermann watched as a single energy strand formed around the damaged ship, then both sped into the darkness and out of visual range in only moments.

"Status?"

Harvey at Sciences turned. "Hull damage on the port flank, just a lucky shot on fire control systems. Minor injuries, life support is up to eighty percent, hull polarization holding at fifty-five."

"Tactical tracking the Stiz. They are headed for the system boundary at high speed, sir."

"Engineering reports full sublight available, hyperlight power in about six hours."

"Helm and Nav responding, still sluggish, sir."

"Comm is clear, Captain. Qoearc are well on their way home."

Westermann looked from station to station, seeing anxious questions in many faces. "As soon as I have details regarding Commander Hamilton and the rest of our crew, I'll let you know."

He looked to Tactical. “Stand down from Battle Stations, go to Standby Alert. Call your relief to the Bridge. Comm, get Medical up here for followup on injuries. Commander Sh'zaoqoq.” She turned in her seat. “Good shooting. Well done.”

“Thank you, sir.” Sh'zaoqoq showed a tired, but satisfied, smile.

Five
Final Duties

"Duty Log, Captain Noah Westermann, 031517.12. The report on the loss of Commander Hamilton, Lieutenant Butler, and eight other shuttle crew and landing party members was a shock to everyone. The official cause is listed as 'time-flow anomalies generated by the alien artifact and aggressive enemy action'. Somehow, the words don't tell the real story.

Lori Hamilton was a unique officer. She wasn't driven by rank or privilege, or command of others, but by doing the right thing for her shipmates.

Skip Butler was a brilliant young man with a bright future. According to survivors, he initially saved Commander Hamilton's life with his own sacrifice, during their escape from the station. Gallantry without thought, bravery with selfless concern for others.

The Commander, herself, saw her landing party and surviving shuttle crew safely away from danger before the explosion. More courage shown by someone I once said was too cautious. I guess I just didn't know her as well as I thought. Surely, she will be seriously considered for the Earthfleet Cross. But posthumous medals are not what Earthfleet is about. I seem to recall an ancient poem about pyrrhic victory.

The memorial service was held on the hangar deck, the only place on the ship large enough to accommodate the entire crew. There wasn't a dry eye anywhere, including my own.

There are times in this Service I wonder where we find those who serve, and what they expect when they join Earthfleet. For me, it was the excitement of the unknown and adventure. For officers like Lori Hamilton, I think it was something much different; the opportunity to serve alongside those who might need a hand from time to time, to keep them a bit more grounded.

I know she certainly did that for me."

* * *

Captain's Ready Room, EAS Agincourt...

Westermann pressed the switch, closing out the log entry. The ready room door buzzed. "Come in."

Dr. Kamisori entered. "You asked to see me, Captain."

Westermann nodded. "Have a seat, Doctor."

Kamisori sat, looking a bit tired.

"Status in Sickbay?"

The doctor thought for a moment. "No critical issues, everyone is back on their feet. The effects of the time-flow are dissipating slowly. We're keeping an eye on several of the crew, just in case."

"Such as Commander Sh'zaoqoq? How's she doing?"

"She's fine, Captain. I've given she and Abol three days of medical leave to spend together. They need the bonding time. Their level of fear was off the charts."

"Yet they did their duties as required."

Kamisori said nothing.

"Alright, Doctor, let's talk about the situation here. You're not happy on *Agincourt*."

"That's not exactly true, Captain."

Westermann sighed. "Alright, what is the issue? Is it with me, or something else?"

Kamisori thought for a moment. "The ship is fine. It's a good crew, well integrated and pretty diverse. Personally, I'd like to see more of that diversity, but I understand the crew works best if the majority is of one Race or type."

Westermann waited. "And..."

Kamisori sat straighter. "Permission to speak freely?"

He sighed. "Go ahead."

"You lack confidence. I know you've been on *Agincourt* for three years, and this is your first command. You have a good record. But you chose very carefully among your senior officers, particularly Lori Hamilton, Abol and Thevoss, Xiaoli at Sciences, and myself. They weren't just the best available, they're all experienced. More than you. You use them as a crutch."

Westermann regarded her for a moment. "All captains rely on their senior officers, especially those who are better at their specialties than they are."

"Yes, but instead of using that opportunity to better yourself, you sit back and give orders."

"That's… my job, Doctor."

"No, your job is to become a better person, more skilled in the operation of the ship, and thereby a better commander. That's why you made the mistakes at the pulsar and got us into this mess in the first place."

Westermann took a moment. He could hardly believe what he was hearing. "I see. Alright, I'll accept that for now. What do you suggest?"

"You won't like it."

"Try me."

Kamisori considered. "Make Thevoss your acting First Officer. You can learn a bit of compassion from her. Move up one of your Lieutenants to Tactical and help Thevoss teach them. Shuffle some duties. Set up classes. Teach them what it means to serve aboard a starship like *Agincourt*."

"I think we've all had a dose of that reality in the last few days, Doctor."

"Yes, and now is the time to show what it really means. Use this opportunity to learn how it affected all of the crew, not just the ones on the Bridge. You might be surprised at the level of feeling on this ship right now."

Westermann looked away for a moment, then nodded. "This is your professional opinion, Doctor? That the captain needs a refresher on what it means to be human?"

She considered. "If that's what you want to call it, yes. But it's also a personal observation. You need to grow more into the role of Captain, not just commanding officer."

He nodded again. "Anything else?"

Kamisori pursed her lips in thought. "I'd like to remain on *Agincourt*. You see, I'm learning, too."

"To keep an eye on me?" Westermann grinned slightly.

"Among other things, yes."

Westermann considered. "Very well, Doctor. Your words are taken as given. Your concern is duly noted. I'll do what I can to follow your advice."

She nodded. "Good. Permission to return to duty?"

"Dismissed. And thank you for your candidness."

Now Kamisori nearly smiled. "Anytime, Captain." The door closed softly as she exited.

Westermann sat alone for long minutes, mulling the doctor's words and recent events. Had he really acted so poorly? Wasn't that exactly what he and Lori Hamilton had talked about before all… this?

He punched the intercom button. "Helm, this is the captain. Status?"

"Hyperlight power online sir. System boundary in ten minutes."

"Very well. Prepare for hyperlight. We're going home."

* * *

The station watched as the last vessel pulled away, heading for the system's gravitational boundary and deep space. It extended its sensors once again, catching the instant the ship disappeared into the "other space", gleaning any data it could. Then it was alone again.

The self-repairing systems had done their work. Minimal damage remained, and that could be worked around by protocols. Debris around the station was slowly settling.

The station drew its time-flow effect closer once again, dampening the intensity to the normal level, and trained its sensors on the planet.

Still, from time to time, it aimed instruments into the distant realm beyond. Its programming was flexible enough it could do this as it decided. What it was searching for, it wasn't quite sure. Certainly, it watched for the creators, yet had no information about their expected return. But it had never done that before the others had arrived. The station considered.

It did not have a sense of loneliness, but at the same time, it reviewed and replayed having the other creatures closely by. It was nearly as when the creators where there. And those memories were, if the station could put an emotion to the sensation, pleasant.

At last it turned again to the planet. Perhaps in time life would arise there. Then the station would not be alone after all.

REBEL AND PROUD

Starship Pheidippides

By

Dennis Young

Prologue

The fiery streak across the planet's sky lit the desert below, washing out the stars. To an observer, had there been anyone other than indigenous animals and a few hardy plants in the area, it appeared whatever was causing the phenomenon would soon impact the ground with considerable force. Possibly enough to cause substantial damage, if there'd been anything but dirt and rock and stony hills nearby.

Fortunately, it didn't happen that way. The object slowed as it neared the barren wastes and came down much more gently than its approach suggested. This would indicate, to the non-existent observers, it was under control of some sort. Possibly even intelligence.

The glow faded as the thing hovered, raised dust, and blew scrub and dirt about. Then touched down almost carefully onto the desert floor with barely a sound. Then silence.

The object cooled. Dust settled. Quiet returned.

It was obviously artificial, not a meteor. Light shone from within as a ramp extended and three figures emerged. They were bipedal and upright, clothed in heavy suits of some type. They surveyed the surroundings, then reentered the object. The ramp closed.

Had the hypothetical outside observer been fluent in language called Earth English, they might have glimpsed the script on the upper surface of the object. It read "PHEIDIPPIDES, EA-9102".

One
Dirtside

"Duty Log, Lieutenant Commander Jennifer Murphy, 120517.18. Pheidippides is currently marooned on a planet… name unknown at this time, I'll look it up. A total systems failure lasting nearly six hours almost killed my entire crew, and by the time we got emergency systems working, three were in sickbay. We sent a Mayday distress call, but I have no idea if it was heard by anyone. Currently Engineering is working on getting us back in space and headed to Fleet Base Twenty-three for repairs.

"I can't stress enough my utter contempt for the Kyniska-class scout design. Not only are these ships cramped and uncomfortable, they're simply dangerous. They may be the fastest things in the Fleet, but that doesn't help much when you're dead."

* * *

EAS Pheidippides…

There's no reason for this, thought Lt. Commander Jenni Murphy.

But orders were orders, right?

She rolled the hardcopy flimsy into a ball and threw it against the bulkhead of her quarters. Her far-too-small-and-cramped "captain's quarters", stuffed between the Bridge and the Head in the tiny *Kyniska*-class scout. Quarters that stank of the previous occupant, a commander who not only bathed too infrequently, but smoked a pipe; an antiquated tobacco pipe, for Cripe's sake! Besides being against regs, it was a filthy, disgusting habit, one cultivated by people who had no concept of ancient diseases. Like lung cancer. And emphysema. And

COPD. Names of things hardly ever heard of in twenty-fifth century medicine. Murphy only knew them because she'd flunked out of med school.

She punched the intercom button. "Murphy to Engineering. Taylor, how much longer before we can get this hunk of junk back in space?"

"Two hours before we can even do a systems check, Murphy. Last time you asked, it was three. Give it a rest, will you? There are only three of us who know enough about phase coils to not blow up the ship when we lift from this dirtball."

She sighed. "Just get it done. We've received new orders and I've got to round up everyone else. I just hope Martin and Jia-Lan aren't in some cave playing 'hide the zucchini'." She heard a snicker before she broke the link.

Murphy stood, her fiery non-reg-length hair brushing the curve of the ceiling, as she turned and headed for the Bridge. She was tall for an Earthfleet officer, topping a hundred ninety centimeters (or as her father liked to say, six-foot-four) and long-boned, typical of her low gravity home planet. She'd been tagged as a pro basketball prospect until she cold-cocked an opponent in an academy game and gotten tossed off the cadet team. Six months of anger management therapy had taken the edge off her volatile temper, and she'd become close friends with her therapist. He was one of only three people she kept in touch with… way out here on the wild frontier.

Where absolutely nothing ever happens, she thought, entering the Bridge and taking her command seat. The only other occupant was Lieutenant Honley, the comm relief/damage control/security officer. On a ship with a crew of only fourteen, multiple hats were worn by everyone.

She took a deep breath. "Chuck, send out a general recall. Apparently, Earthfleet has found real work for us to do."

* * *

"OK, crew, listen up. Fleet Base Twenty-three has an anomaly they want us to check out about three light years from here. Weak signal, unknown origin, and damn close to the Qoearc border."

Murphy stood in the center of a circle of faces, the shade of *Pheidippides* protecting them from the intense heat of the local sun. They met outdoors, as there was no room in the ship for the crew to assemble. "I need a status report from all departments in thirty minutes, and this bird has to be in space by 1800 Hours."

A collective groan made its way around the crowd. Murphy looked at Taylor Thomas, her Engineer. "We're going to need full hyperlight capability by then, too."

Thomas shook his head. "No way, Captain. Maybe by tomorrow, but for now, 60c is the best we can do. Phase coils are still not in full tune."

"How much time if we stay dirtside?"

Thomas pursed his lips and looked away for a moment. "Six hours, no less. Maybe more."

"You've got three. Get on it." Murphy motioned to the hatchway. Thomas took his techs in tow and disappeared into the ship. "Anything else I need to know before we get our hands dirty?"

"Nearly fifty percent of the main circuit breakers are burned out, Captain," replied Sar Ch'rehrin, her Arnec First Officer. "We have adequate spares, but it will take two hours for full replacement."

Murphy nodded. "Take whoever you need for help and get it done. Taylor and his techs will be busy in Engineering, so it's your baby. Once that's in the works, get busy on tracking down this anomaly. I sent a copy of the fleettext to your station."

Ch'rehrin nodded, then looked to Steven Allworth and Jorge Trujillo, Helm/Nav officers. "Gentlemen, with me." The trio followed the engineers up the ramp.

Murphy looked to the remaining crew. "What else?"

"Karen and I worked the bugs out of the Helm and Nav systems," said Jules O'Brien. "It passed full diagnostics about an hour ago."

Murphy nodded. "Get your reports ready for review and meet back out here. Thirty minutes. We can't keep the admirals waiting."

* * *

"The thrusters don't have enough power to lift us into orbit, but we can hover and light the sublight engines about five hundred meters off the ground." Tony Ball, one of two engineering techs, passed his PADD to Murphy in her command seat. "That should be high enough to not start fires."

"There's really nothing to burn, Tony. It's a desert out there, in case you hadn't noticed." Murphy wiped sweat from her forehead. The environmental system had shown further glitches and had been shut down during maintenance. It had only come back online in the last twenty minutes.

"Agreed, but still… Prime Directive and all that."

"Noted. Do what you can. We lift off in one hour." Murphy turned to Ch'rehrin at the Sciences console. "Tell me some good news. Are we space-worthy?"

"We will be within parameters by launch time." Ch'rehrin glanced to Murphy. "May I suggest you take the opportunity for a shower?"

"Do I smell that bad?" Murphy chuckled. "Alright, you have the Conn. I'll be back in thirty minutes."

"Captain." Martin Teng-Hey motioned from his Comm station. "I'm picking up encrypted signals from orbit. The analyzer says it may be Qoearc."

Murphy sighed. "Confirm and advise." She glanced to the Tactical station. "Hatu, is everyone on board?"

"All hands accounted for." Hatu Gil's Latino English was quick in reply.

Murphy looked again to her science officer. "Cripes, this is just what we need. Please say it's not a battle cruiser."

Ch'rehrin scanned his instruments for a moment, then read codes from a screen. "Low mass, likely a scout, maybe an escort of some sort. The planet is about to occlude it… now."

"Then let's get out of here." Murphy punched the intercom. "Engineering, Bridge. Taylor, we've got Qoearc company in orbit, just went to the other side of the planet. We've got about thirty minutes to clean up and get out of here. Status?"

Voices beyond the Engineering pickup argued as Murphy waited. *"We can lift, but 70c max. Sorry, Captain."*

"Gonna have to be good enough. Hang on back there, this could be bumpy. Helm, Nav, get us out of here as quickly as possible. If they swing around and scan the surface, they'll have us in a heartbeat. Punch it."

* * *

Pheidippides rose slowly on thruster power only, sank back toward the ground, then rose again as Murphy ordered sublight at ten percent a thousand meters off the surface. Dust blew nearly that high as the ship gained altitude. They left behind a crater of fused glass nearly a kilometer wide.

"Damn it, Conn, what happened?"

"Sorry, Captain, the thrusters cut out and I had no choice. If you hadn't ordered sublight engines, we'd be in a heap on the ground right now." O'Brien looked over his shoulder with a guilty glance. "You said punch it."

"Bridge, Engineering. No damage, Hyperlight power through Sixty available at your command."

"Helm is answering, Captain, navigation clear. We made orbit with five minutes to spare."

"Keep us out of the Qoearc's sight. Tactical, what have you got?"

"Ion trail around the planet as expected, emergence in maybe ten minutes, fifteen at most. Depends on their orbit altitude."

"Ch'rehrin, did they follow us here?"

"Probably to watch us crash," muttered Karen Connor at the Nav station.

Ch'rehrin turned from his screens. "Impossible to say, however, our entry trail through the atmosphere was likely visible to a Qoearc scout's sensors, assuming they were within five million kilometers."

"Meaning they were either following us or an amazing coincidence." Murphy let out a heavy breath. "Never mind. Alright, back to the mission. Helm, course to investigate the anomaly, and once we're clear of the system singularity, get us out of here, maximum hyperlight."

"Captain, we have divergent readings in the tactical system."

"Damn, Hatu, I thought you had that fixed!"

"Bridge, Engineering. We've got a wobble in the phase coils."

Murphy hit the intercom switch. "Meaning?"

"We can't go to hyperlight… yet."

"Time to repair?"

"Geez, Murphy, we don't even know what the problem is. Give me ten minutes."

"Captain."

Murphy turned to Ch'rehrin's soft voice and calm face. She nodded, drew a breath, and sat straighter. "Taylor, get on it and let me know as soon as you have a fix." She clicked off. "Alright, people, let's see what we can do. Helm, keep us out of sight, Nav, get me a projection of the Qoearc's orbit as soon as you can. Don't we have a few drones aboard?"

"Three, Captain," replied Connor at Nav. She punched up a display quickly. "We have one loaded in the launch tube now that we were going to use once we reached the anomaly."

"Good. Launch when ready, we'll use it to peek around the planet and find the Qoearc when they're out of our scanning range."

"Captain, I have the analysis of the anomaly as you requested. I'm sending to your PADD."

Murphy glanced at the screen beside her. "So, Fleet wants us to investigate a possible Qoearc mining operation?"

"It would seem so."

"Bridge, Engineering. We're ready to go any time."

Murphy punched the intercom button. "Status?"

Thomas's voice carried chagrin. "*My fault, I hit a kill-switch by accident. Took one of the phase coils offline, which caused a red light. Sorry.*"

Murphy caught Ch'rehrin's glance. "Understood, Taylor. We're all a bit stressed right now. Glad you caught it. Prepare for hyperlight on my command."

"*Aye, Captain.*"

"Ms. Connor, is that probe still in the launch tube?"

"Yes, Captain."

"Cancel launch, then. Mr. O'Brien, take us out of orbit, full sublight. Keep the planet between us and the Qoearc. Go to hyperlight as soon as we're clear of the singularity. Get us the hell out of here."

* * *

Murphy was alone in the galley when Ulyana Melinkov, the ship's doctor, entered.

Melinkov was old-school Russian, from the Mother Country itself, and could be aloof if approached with rank in mind. Other times, she was almost motherly, especially with a crew of young officers, none of which, other than the exec and herself, were more than three or four years out of the academy. Melinkov was well into her second decade in Earthfleet.

Pheidippides, she knew, was the first deep space assignment for several on board, and scout ship duty could be boring, if not downright depressing. Her office was always open for a chat, a game of chess, or if necessary, a venting session.

Melinkov drew a cup of hot tea from the dispenser and sat across from Murphy, whose eyes were vacant and introspective. "You are having a better day, now we are on the way to our assignment?" The doctor's Russian inflection was usually almost nonexistent, but at times could be used as a drawing-out strategy.

Murphy's eyes focused and she grinned wryly. "Does it show that much?"

"No. Just rumors, something about a shouting match on the Bridge. I give such things little thought, however."

Murphy shook her head. "No, you don't. Okay, Doc, I blew up at Hatu. My error, and I apologized. I blew up at Taylor in Engineering and apologized. I'm human. Sue me."

Melinkov sipped. "Mm. You are also the captain, yes?"

Murphy rolled her eyes. "Don't give me this crap again, Doc. I have a temper. I also have pretty good leadership ability. I just get..."

Melinkov set down her cup. "Frustrated? Angry? Enraged?"

Murphy sighed. "Let's leave it at frustrated. Yes, I get very frustrated because I can't... control everything. I can't... help."

"Would it help if you gave the control to those who can help? Or would this make you feel as though you are... quitting?"

Murphy shrugged and said nothing.

"Tell me why you are in Earthfleet."

"Working up your psyche report, Doc?"

"Possibly. What would you say regarding your last thirty-day performance?" Melinkov drank and refilled her cup. She drew a second and set it in front of Murphy.

"I'd say about a D-plus."

"That high?" Melinkov watched Murphy for a moment. "Can you tell me what is frustrating you, specifically?"

Murphy waved a hand. "Well, how about the ship falling apart around us for starters? Then we've had only one assignment in the last, what, sixty days? Then we almost crash on a planet I still haven't found on the charts. Now we have a Qoearc who might be tracking us." She drank, nearly draining her cup. "Shall I go on?"

"So… you are bored?"

Murphy looked away. "This is a scout. That's all we do, scout. We don't have any scientific equipment for exploring, there are no recreational areas on board, unless you count the bunks, and our library is a year out of date." She huffed a breath. "And on top of that, there's been nothing to scout! Yeah, I'm bored. The crew is bored, you're bored, the whole damn ship is bored."

She finished her cup. "This ship hasn't had a refit in nearly two years. We haven't had R&R in almost eight months, unless you count our crash-landing. There are only fourteen people on this ship. You know how tough it is to have a social life when your entire crew is fourteen people, most of whom want off this ship as much as I do?"

"So this is Earthfleet's fault, your assignment?"

Murphy stared. "When, exactly, did I say that?"

"Over the last few minutes, you have certainly pointed fingers at everyone but yourself… Captain."

"So, I'm to blame for all this?"

Melinkov shrugged and nodded at the same time. "It would seem the captain is to be the first to accept responsibility for the ship. Does it not say so in Earthfleet Regulations?"

"I don't believe what I'm hearing," Murphy mumbled.

"This is certainly not the first time we have spoken of this, yes? Every time, you say the same things. You are not happy in Earthfleet? You do not want the responsibility of being the captain?" Melinkov paused. "Perhaps, if you are unable to perform duties of the captaincy, you should relieve yourself and turn over command to your executive."

Murphy swallowed, growing angrier by the minute. "Is that a threat, Doctor?"

"An observation, Captain. One you should take to heart. It is time, is it not?" She drank again. "In my opinion, you are looking at that D-plus and wondering how to raise it, while not wanting to do the necessary things to do so. You cannot transfer off the ship, you cannot control the Qoearc, you cannot change the nature of your orders. What, then, can you do? Where is your control? If you are the captain, it should be obvious."

"Is that a medical evaluation?"

Melinkov pursed her lips. "Call it what you will. How long until we reach wherever it is we are going?"

Murphy thought for a moment. "About five days, why?"

"Then my suggestion, as your doctor, would be to focus your energies on positive steps until time for our scouting to be done. What can you accomplish in five days with a ship you say is falling apart and a crew who is bored?"

Murphy toyed with her cup. "Maybe we should throw a party. A 'we didn't crash and die' party." She gave a self-depreciating laugh.

"An excellent idea. And perhaps an opportunity to make *Pheidippides*… what is the term… 'ship-shape' again?"

"Work, to give everyone something else to gripe about?"

Melinkov raised her face. "Work to give a sense of purpose, and of being in Earthfleet together."

She collected the cups and set them in the recycler, then turned to Murphy. "I am glad we had this opportunity to talk, Captain. Your ideas are worthy, and I will be proud to be part of your coming plans."

* * *

"Duty Log, Lieutenant Commander Jennifer Murphy, 121017.08. Four days ago, we held a "We Didn't Crash and Die" dinner, after our forced landing on an unnamed planet. With excellent foresight, my First Officer's quick survey during our planetside stay, and subsequent system study, showed it to be a suitable, if marginal, Class M world worth further investigation. He has sent a subspace squirt back to Fleet Base Twenty-three with the information.

"Further, in the five days travel to our assignment destination, the crew has been busy with repairs, refurbishments, and what upgrading we can do with our meager onboard supplies. But I'm happy to report, Pheidippides is in much better shape than she was before our emergency event. I'm thinking about another party to celebrate."

* * *

"Assignment coordinates in thirty seconds, Captain." Ch'rehrin turned to his panel, then once more to the main viewer as Murphy waited in her command seat. "Benchmark… now."

"Disengage hyperlight, Mr. O'Brien, bring us to rest relative to the anomaly position. Thrusters to station-keeping." Murphy pressed the intercom button. "Engineering, Bridge. Status, Taylor?"

"Captain, Chief Taylor is off duty, this is Lieutenant Ball. Engineering systems are nominal, phase coils decoupled and cooling normally."

"Stand down from hyperlight, but be prepared to go at a moment's notice if we pick up any perimeter ships." Murphy clicked off and looked around the cramped Bridge. Everyone and everything seemed orderly. "Mr. Ch'rehrin, where are we?"

"Less than one-quarter light year from the established Qoearc Interdiction Zone, Captain. The closest star is a red dwarf in Qoearc space, approximately two light years to galactic north. The star has four planets, none habitable, and a Qoearc surveillance base known to have at least three scout-class craft that patrol the border regularly."

Murphy looked to Hatu Gil at Tactical. "Scan long and short range, look for anything stealthed, Mr. Gil. Karen, what's on the Nav scanners?"

"There's a free-floater about a half light year on the Qoearc side of the border, with a trailing tail of asteroids. It's floating slowly parallel to the demarcation area. Other than that, next to nothing."

"Likely the Qoearc are mining the trailing asteroids, Captain," said Ch'rehrin. "Much easier than the planet itself."

"Doesn't Fleet have this info? If they do, why are we here?"

Ch'rehrin stepped from his post to Murphy's side. "I suggest it is time to open the sealed orders, Captain."

She gave him a look. "I did that already. Let's meet in the conference niche to review yours." She rose. "Jules, you have the Conn, call your second to the Bridge. I don't want any stations unmanned for a while."

Murphy led Ch'rehrin through the doors to the sound of O'Brien's voice on the comm to his relief.

* * *

Ch'rehrin passed his PADD to Murphy as they entered the tiny office and sealed the door. She tapped in her authentication code and handed it back, then sat, waiting as he decrypted the orders and read the message.

"The Qoearc are suspected of using the asteroids as monitoring stations themselves, rather than bringing more ships into the area, which would raise the concerns of Earthfleet," Ch'rehrin began. "Any sizeable collection of ships in this remote area might then be construed as a threat, possibly even a prelude to incursion."

Murphy shook her head. "Why the big deal then? If Fleet knows this, why is it worth an encrypted message labeled Level Ten, Eyes Only? Yes, it's our job to be sneaky, but this…"

Ch'rehrin considered, his near-black eyes unreadable, as all Arneci were. "We become the monitoring station, therefore. We will likely receive additional orders once we have reported our current findings. We may be required to follow the free-floating planet and report on Qoearc activity."

Murphy rose from her chair and poured tea for both of them, then sat again. She drank, musing. "No, there's something more. Something they're not telling us, even in a fully encrypted 'if you look at this, we'll have to kill you' message. They want us in the area for another reason. What?"

She pressed the intercom switch. "Tactical, Captain. Hatu, slave your sensors to Nav and work with Karen to look for anything within…" She paused, looking to Ch'rehrin. He showed three fingers. "Three light years on this side of the border."

"Three light years, aye. What are we looking for, Captain?"

"Anything at all out of the ordinary. Signals, unusual masses, space junk..." She paused again, thinking. "Or nothing at all. Maybe a void, like a stealthed ship. Nothing where there should be something."

"I don't understand, but we'll do what we can. Tactical out."

"You are becoming adept at saying something while saying nothing, Captain." Ch'rehrin almost smiled.

Murphy shrugged. "Like our orders? There's something they're not telling us, so we have to find out what it is ourselves. Something so important, they couldn't even put it in sealed orders, fearing it would be intercepted and decrypted. But they had to hide it in a real set of orders that made sense in case those were intercepted."

"Double-think?"

Murphy shrugged. "Fleet paranoia, circular thinking. And since when is Fleet logical?"

Ch'rehrin considered, then nodded. "What then are our actual orders?"

Murphy emptied her cup, then looked up in realization. "Not Qoearc hanky-panky, not a new free-floater, and sure as hell not a Qoearc mining expedition. Something they wanted us to search for once we were in the neighborhood. The orders are a map. A treasure map."

* * *

Murphy ordered the Tactical and Nav relief officers to organize a plan for monitoring the Qoearc as *Pheidippides* paced the planet. She told them it was part of their onboard training. Hatu Gil and Karen Connor were then given private instructions to work with Ch'rehrin and search for specifics in the vicinity, as ordered earlier.

"But more," explained Murphy, meeting with the three in the conference niche again. Two were company; four were a crowd, with Gil and Ch'rehrin standing behind Conner, and Murphy seated at the desk. "I want to know what's not right about this area. We have orders to monitor the Qoearc, which your relief is doing now. I want the three of you to find out what's unusual on this side of the border while the Qoearc watch us watch them."

Again, the door was sealed, and Murphy had showered, dressed in a fresh jumpsuit uniform, and actually put her hair into a semi-formal ponytail. Since her dressing-down by the doctor, she'd done her best to look the part of a ship captain. She wasn't entirely comfortable with it, but as pointed out by Melinkov, it was her job.

"So… what exactly are we looking for, Captain? Can you give us a hint?" Connor passed a look for support to Gil, who only shrugged.

"No, I can't." Murphy's eyes met Ch'rehrin's for an instant. "Think of it as a treasure hunt. Easter eggs. Christmas presents hidden in your parents' closet."

"I understood that reference," said Gil. Connor, having been born and reared on Marsopolis in a totally different culture, only shook her head.

Murphy grinned. "Earth culture, Karen, religious holidays. I did a minor at Academy in Earth History. You might check them out some time."

She looked back to Gil. "Continue to work with your seconds, because the Qoearc detail is the real thing as well. We need all the info we can get on their activities, and not just the mining. Have your relief watch for ships, unusual movement, possible incursions into Earth Alliance space, the typical close-watch stuff we do. Keep them busy while you and the first officer do the dirty work."

Murphy looked to them both. "Questions? Okay, report to Lieutenant Ch'rehrin every four hours or as needed. Anything odd, let him know. Let's get to it."

Gil and Connor edged out of the tiny space and Ch'rehrin waited at the door, then closed and sealed it again. "What is next, Captain?"

Murphy shook her head. "You have no idea how uncomfortable I am with giving orders. I feel like I'm telling people who already know their jobs what to do."

"As I understand," said Ch'rehrin, as he sat, "part of a captain's work is to remind others of theirs. Not to do it for them, but to see it done. I believe the Earth term is... 'mother hen'."

"Cripes, my first officer is a comedian." Murphy chuckled as Ch'rehrin only watched. She sat back, quiet for a moment. "Thoughts? Maybe Qoearc poking around? Stiz, although I can't imagine them being interested in a cold free-floater? Something else? Someone else?"

"We will know more within a day or two, perhaps. If nothing then, I suggest we expand our search or reposition the ship. However, we continue the charade of monitoring the Qoearc, regardless, correct?"

"I agree. Make them keep their eyes on us. What about the ship following us to the planet? Any further developments?"

Ch'rehrin looked up. "I will add that to the relief crew assignment. My apologies, I neglected to follow up, once we left orbit."

"See to it. Maybe wherever they went might give us a clue or two as to what we're really looking for."

* * *

"Bridge to Captain. I think we've got something."

Hatu Gil's voice on the intercom broke into Murphy's subconscious. She rolled over in her bunk and missed the intercom button twice before hitting it. "Sleeping, give me a minute."

She sat up, head in her hands, and let her mind clear slowly. The dream had been as vivid as any she'd had in weeks, and she willed her emotions to ebb. She knew she needed to talk to the doctor about the recurring images, but simply hadn't had the guts to do it.

She rubbed her eyes and shook hair out of her face. "Okay, I'm awake. What have you got?"

"Just an OC matter, but I thought we'd discuss when you're due on the Bridge. It came in ten minutes ago."

Cripes! OC! She took a deep breath before she replied. "In the conference room, fifteen minutes." She clicked off and fell back into her bunk. *OC! Ordo Capitellum,* Capital Order from the Latin. Nothing in Earthfleet was higher!

She shed her oversized night shirt and ran the sonic cleaner over herself quickly, slid into her jumpsuit, and took thirty seconds to brush her hair and tie it back. Her mind raced. *Treasure hunt, indeed.*

"Melinkov to Captain Murphy. May we meet in my office when you have time?"

Murphy hit the intercom again. "Sure. What's up?"

"A matter needing your attention soonest."

That's about as vague and scary as it gets. "I have a conference in ten minutes. When that's done, I'll come by Sickbay."

"Very well. Thank you, Captain."

Murphy knew when Melinkov became coldly formal, it wasn't a good sign. *Oh, well. One crisis at a time.*

She took a final look in the mirror, decided she looked important enough, and headed out the door for the short walk to the conference niche.

* * *

If it was even possible, the room was more crowded than before. With Murphy at the desk, Ch'rehrin beside her, Gil and Connor, and now Martin Teng-Hey from Comm standing at the door, it was nearly impossible to move. She considered folding the desk up, but they needed the screen to project onto the wall behind her.

Murphy was on her second cup of tea. "All right, what have we found?"

"The OC was received and decrypted immediately, providing new coordinates for investigation, nothing more", replied Ch'rehrin. "Lieutenant Gil will explain, Captain. I received only a summary."

Murphy's eyes moved to the tactical officer. "You're on, Lieutenant."

The screen lit. "You asked for us to search for something, then you mentioned 'nothing', which stuck with me. We did a full sweep with HI sensors, particle assessment, mass analyzers, everything we could think of. Nothing out of the ordinary came up."

"… And then?"

Gil adjusted the focus on the image and zoomed in on a smaller area, nearly smiling at Murphy's sardonic tone. "We started looking for nothing. Dark energy, dark matter, dark anything at all, neutrino trails, anti-protons, negative mass, vacuum energy. And we found it."

The screen changed to an asteroid, roughly oval, pocked with ancient strikes from others of its kind. "The rock is about two hundred kilometers long and a hundred fifty wide. Big thing, but it masses too much for its rocky content. Something else is there. Something big."

"Estimates on the ancillary mass, Lieutenant?" asked Ch'rehrin.

"Three to five hundred thousand kilos, Commander. Hard to tell exactly at this distance, but something very substantial."

Murphy turned from the image back to the crowd before her. "How far, Mr. Gil?"

"Half a light year, slightly more. I seriously doubt the Qoearc are aware of it because it's simply not something anyone sane would look for."

"Thank you for suggesting your captain is nuts," said Murphy, showing a crooked grin. "Well done. Really, very well done. Okay, what else?"

"A very weak signal, Captain," said Teng-Hey. "Once Mr. Gil and Ms. Connor pinpointed the location, we trained everything we had on the source."

The room was quiet for a moment. "Don't keep us in suspense, Lieutenant. What did you hear?"

Teng-Hey began to speak, then paused, took a breath, and continued. "Ancient code, several hundred years old. But confirmed as Earth origin. And so heavily encrypted, we can't even imagine what it says."

"Then how did you identify it as Earth origin, Lieutenant?" asked Ch'rehrin. "And how did you determine its age?"

"Part of the signal is in clear, sir, or I should say, Earth English, in fact. Old Morse Code. Dot-dot-dot, dash-dash-dash, dot-dot-dot."

"SOS," breathed Connor. "It's a distress signal."

"Holy crap," said Murphy.

Two
Unexpected Findings

"Duty Log, Lieutenant Commander Jennifer Murphy, 120717.19. We've sneaked away from the border area, and so far, no Qoearc are following. There is also no sign of the vessel seen at the planet, so for the moment, we're clear to continue the mission without interference.

"We have no idea what we'll find when we arrive at the target coordinates in about eight hours, but I'll order Standby Alert before we drop out of hyperlight. Our approach will be cautious, to say the least. For Fleet to send us on an OC says either they have enormous confidence in us, or we're simply the only ship available. Of course, the third option is, we're expendable, and if we don't survive whatever we've been ordered to investigate, they'll know to send a bigger ship next time."

* * *

EAS Pheidippides…

Murphy sat with Doctor Melinkov in her sickbay office. A hardcopy of Ensign Jia-Lan Wèi's file rested on the desk. Murphy closed the cover and sighed. "How far along?"

"Six to eight weeks. She is perfectly healthy, Captain, and I see no reason for her to be denied duties."

Murphy nodded. "I don't doubt her ability Doc, I just…" She sat back for a long moment, lost in thought. She looked up after a moment. "Martin?"

Melinkov nodded. "She had not yet told him, and I have left it up to her to do so."

"Once they've… talked, I want to meet with them and you, to decide how to handle this."

Melinkov shook her head. "There is no special treatment necessary, Captain. It is life, and this is not the first ship to have a pregnant woman as a crew member."

"No, just the first one with only a crew of fourteen, nearly three months from a base, on an OC mission. Happens every day, right?"

Melinkov nodded again. "Your point is taken. Do you have any thought how long the investigation will take?"

"None. It could be days, it could be months. You might be delivering a baby before we're done."

"Our facilities are adequate. Again, it is life, and life happens in its own way. I may assist, but it will come, regardless."

Murphy thought for a moment. "What about medical stasis?"

Melinkov gave her a stern look. "You would have me put the Ensign in stasis for what reason?"

"Safety of the mother and unborn child, if nothing else, Doc."

"Leaving you a crew manifest short a member for an important mission."

Murphy shrugged. "We can manage. It's not something I'd want to make an order—"

"Then do not do so. Captain, this is not a disease and will not affect the Ensign's performance of her duties."

"Until she gets so round, she can hardly walk."

Melinkov pursed her lips. "Let us be patient and see how matters go with the mission first. At the very least, she is fully capable for six months."

Murphy tapped the folder in front of her. "No security duties, period. No off-ship excursions, no cargo duties, no damage control duties after the first trimester."

Melinkov nodded. "Agreed, Captain, and prudent. I am certain you will find plenty of work for the Ensign otherwise. However, regular exercise is advised for the health of mother and child."

"Alright, Doc, if you say so. Cripes, this isn't anything we needed right now."

"But it has come, and a cause for joy, yes? A new life into the universe, unique and fresh."

Murphy grinned wryly. "You should write some poetry about it, Doc. You have a way with words."

Melinkov showed a slight smile. "What makes you think I have not already?"

* * *

"Hyperlight emergence benchmark coming up, Captain." Jorge Trujillo, the second-shift Nav officer, turned to Murphy in her command seat. "One minute."

"Mr. Ch'rehrin, full passive sensors. I don't want to disturb whatever this thing is if it's asleep. Tactical, keep your eyes open for other ships."

A chorus of acknowledgements met Murphy's weary ears. She had been on the Bridge for nearly twelve hours without a break and was running on caffeine and a stim-shot administered by Dr. Melinkov six hours earlier. It was wearing off, and she considered requesting another.

"Thirty seconds, Captain," said Ch'rehrin, watching his screens. "Mark".

"Disengage hyperlight, Helm, bring us to rest regarding the asteroid, take us to one hundred kilometers relative distance."

"Aye, Captain, one hundred kilometers."

"Mr. Ch'rehrin?" Murphy turned to face the science station.

"Scanning… no sign of the object yet."

"Tactical?"

Lieutenant Demarcy, Hatu Gil's relief, shook his head. "Clear space, Captain, just us and the big rock."

Murphy hit the intercom. "Engineering, Bridge. Taylor, status."

"Board is green, phase coils currently on standby, we can go to hyperlight on your command."

"Keep the engines hot just in case." She clicked off. "Mr. Ch'rehrin?"

"Still nothing, Captain."

"Detection," said Demarcy from Tactical. "Something coming up from the other side, possibly stealthed."

Murphy looked at her chair arm telltales; yes, she'd ordered Standby Alert, even in her fatigue. "Eyes, Tactical, passive only," she reminded the lieutenant.

"Captain, there is certainly something in orbit around the asteroid, but heavily masked," said Ch'rehrin. "I cannot identify the object directly, only by its absence."

"As Lieutenant Gil suggested, nothing, not something." Murphy glanced one to the other. "Suggestion?"

Ch'rehrin turned. "There is no energy output other than the continuing signal detected before, the distress call, and very weak. I do not understand how the object cannot be seen directly."

"Reflective panels," said Demarcy suddenly, then he faced Murphy. "Old-school stuff, really old, and completely passive. Mirrors, Captain."

"Reflecting nothing but stars back at us, so we can't see it directly." Trujillo at Nav whistled. "Brilliant."

"Mr. Ch'rehrin, confirm, please." Murphy turned back to the main viewer and the image of the slowly-tumbling asteroid. "Helm, move us in carefully. Thrusters only."

"Aye, Captain."

"Confirmed. I'm detecting reflections of star patterns from a point source in orbit about the asteroid." Ch'rehrin turned to Murphy. "Orbital period approximately thirty-eight minutes, currently five minutes into the passage."

"Helm, adjust to follow, put our orbit parallel to the object ten kilometers out. Hold with thrusters only."

"A pretty good balancing act, Captain, but I can manage," replied Steven Allworth, the relief helm officer.

Murphy looked to Demarcy again. "Anything?"

"Dead, Captain, just—"

All the Bridge lights went out. Panels went dark, the screen blanked, Murphy could hear the environmental system fans slowing and stopping. Gravity slowly ebbed from her body.

For ten seconds, the Bridge was eerily quiet. Five seconds later, the deep red emergency lights came on. Several loose objects were retrieved by crew before they could float too far from the control panels.

"Seat restraints," said Murphy quietly, as she clicked the intercom switch. "Engineering, Bridge. Taylor, what's going on?" The speaker was silent. Murphy clicked her wrist communicator. "Taylor, Murphy. What happened?"

"Taylor here. Engineering is dead, everything just... stopped. No engines, no power, nothing."

"What caused it? Same thing as before?"

"Captain, I have no idea, but it's not shipboard. Even if the hyperlight core was jettisoned, we'd still have the sublight engines for ship's power."

"How much emergency power do we have?"

"About six hours. We can extend that to ten or more if we cut back in a few places."

"Do it. I'll get back to you." Murphy looked to Ch'rehrin working with a hand-held scanner. "Anything?"

"The ship is dead, Captain, and there are residual indications of a dampening field of some sort."

"EMP," said Demarcy. "I caught a whiff of it on scanners just before everything went out."

"From the object?"

Demarcy nodded. "Most likely, as that's the only other thing around."

"Ch'rehrin, get all departments on your wrist comm and have them check in, make sure everyone is aware and okay. Mr. Demarcy, use your aux-scanner and see what you can find."

"Captain, I suggest we go EVA for less interference from the ship's hull." Ch'rehrin now stood at Murphy's side, speaking softly, holding the chair arm to remain stationary.

"Alright, but take someone with you, one of the E-techs. Don't get yourself lost out there." She watched as Ch'rehrin took his exit, stopping at the door to engage the manual operator.

Murphy waited. All around the tiny Bridge, the crew used their hand-held scanners to monitor whatever they could. The emergency lights soon became depressing, until Murphy ordered them dampened.

"Captain, we're drifting," said Allworth at the helm. "Hard to say how much, but away from the asteroid at least."

Murphy nodded wordlessly, watching the blank screen. She knew her ship was in serious trouble, but couldn't think of anything to do but stay calm and wait.

Her wristcom buzzed. *"Bridge, Engineering. Murphy, we've got a bit of power restored. Whatever it was, the effect seems to be fading."*

She pressed the reply button. "Stay put, don't do anything drastic. The first officer and one of your E-techs are outside seeing if they can get a better look."

"Got it. We'll sit tight."

"Ch'rehrin here. We are exiting the outer lock. Stand by."

Sounds of breathing came through Murphy's wrist comm as she waited.

"Ch'rehrin, Captain. The effect is confirmed from the object, which we can see more clearly from here. Likely it was an automated defense system, engaged by our proximity. Effects seem to be fading."

"Noted, get back inside. Engineering reports the ship is coming back to life."

"I'm also detecting a faint neutrino source."

"From the object?"

"From beyond this vicinity. Possibly another ship."

Murphy frowned. "Alright, return to the airlock and stand by. As soon as we have the helm, I'm getting us away from this thing. We'll confer as soon as we can."

She punched the button, not waiting for Ch'rehrin's reply, and sat back. *Cripes!*

* * *

Murphy called another conference, this one by comm, once the ship's power had been restored. She ordered *Pheidippides* moved a thousand klicks beyond the asteroid, and alarms set in case other EMP's were detected, at which time the ship's polarization would automatically reverse. She wasn't sure if it would do any good against an electromagnetic pulse, but anything was better than nothing.

"Status?" Murphy sat in her command seat, still fatigued, but more alert from Dr. Melinkov's second stims-shot. Ch'rehrin and Hatu Gil stood before her, the other stations manned by their primaries. Both tactical stations were manned and operating.

"Full power restored, Captain, no damage detected," said Thomas from the intercom. *"We had to reset half the circuit breakers, though, and replace a few more."*

Murphy looked to her first officer.

"The object masses nearly five hundred thousand kilos, Captain, and as seen, is shielded by reflective panels, most of which are still intact."

"Most. But not all." Murphy's eyes drifted to the screen and the asteroid showing there. "How do we get close enough to see if there are any identifying marks or registry numbers without endangering the ship?"

"Skiff?" Gil shrugged at Murphy's glance. "If we use thrusters, then coast, maybe it won't hit us again."

"A reasonable suggestion," added Ch'rehrin. "But if incorrect, you would crash into the asteroid."

"Thrusters can be set for mechanical use only," said Taylor from Engineering. *"Manually operating the valves requires only a low-power signal. It takes them out of the control loop. It's a safety thing they built in."*

Murphy exchanged glances with Ch'rehrin, then nodded. "Set it up. We have a mission, and unless we do something, we could sit out here for weeks." She sighed. "I'm taking a break. Mr. Ch'rehrin, I suggest you do the same. Mr. Gil, you have the conn, arrange this with

Engineering and we'll continue to observe and monitor for the next six hours. This thing has been out here a long time. It's not going anywhere."

Murphy rose stiffly. "I'll be in Sickbay for a bit, then in quarters. Holler if anything comes up."

She exited, sagging noticeably beyond the door, and pressed her wrist-comm button. "Dr. Melinkov, Murphy. Have Martin and Jia-Lan meet us in your office immediately."

* * *

It's gonna be okay. Murphy stripped off her sweat-stained jumpsuit and tossed it in the recycler, pulled on her nightshirt, and collapsed onto her bunk. The meeting with Jia-Lan and Martin had gone… if not well, at least without anyone shouting or getting thrown in the brig. Not that *Pheidippides* had a brig, but whatever. She'd assured them there would be no restriction of duties, other than as discussed with the doctor, and no repercussions regarding their files. It was life, as Dr. Melinkov had said, and it happened every day. She'd even wished them well, and told them once they were back at base, they'd throw a party for them. Whenever that might be.

Murphy considered. The talk she'd had with the doctor regarding her feelings about Earthfleet kept drifting up. She'd enlisted after flunking out of med school, and they'd tried to put her right back in. But she tested out high in command ability, or as she said, "telling people what to do because I have a loud voice and I'm really tall". Then, boom, she was given a ship right out of Academy. Well, after six months on board a frigate-class ship, directing a rescue operation that could have left half the crew dead, but didn't. She'd even gotten a commendation.

Now, in command of *Pheidippides* for nearly a year, her thoughts were entirely different. She'd remarked often about how small the frigate she served on was. Of course, that was before *Pheidippides* and its crew of fourteen. She knew every one of them damn near as well as she knew her family. Maybe even more so.

I signed on for two years of scout duty. Can I stand another year of this smelly cabin? One more year of seeing no one but these thirteen other people, and weeks of no action, no real life? How the hell do officers get chosen for this type of service?

She glanced at the chronometer. She needed sleep, but the stim-shot was still going full force. She sat up in her bunk and tried to meditate for a bit. No luck. She swung her long legs over the side and closed her eyes. She thought about her sister and brother, both in civilian work and successful in their careers. She thought about her parents, her dad still living, but her mom gone now for over ten years.

Cancer. Even in the twenty-fifth century, it still crops up occasionally, and if not caught, is still a killer. Dammit.

She laid her face in her hands and tried again to relax. Just… relax. At last, she lay down again and pulled the bedcover close, closing her eyes. She sighed.

I miss you, Mom.

* * *

Lieutenant Hatu Gil sat in the command seat, watching the screen and mulling options. Taking the skiff to the object had been an off-the-cuff remark, but not really a bad one. Chief Thomas's suggestion about using manual thrusters was certainly a valid point, and added strength to his suggestion. And like everyone on board, he had no idea what this thing was, how it got here, or what its purpose might be. But he was beginning to have ideas.

First, it was masked, but only passively. Current Earthfleet sensors, especially the ones ships like *Pheidippides* carried, could track stealthed vessels with relative ease. The power output for stealth had made it nearly useless, and stealthing by masking electronics, sublight exhaust, and other dead giveaways were much more efficient now. The old-style mechanical cloaking was a thing of the past, and the improved Qoearc version quickly becoming so.

Gil suspected this object was a prototype of some sort, either a monitoring station—it was certainly large enough to carry a semi-permanent crew—or a weapons testbed. Where better to try it out than a remote part of the I-Zone, where "incidents" occasionally happened and were seldom investigated fully. By either Earthfleet or the Qoearc "Defense Force". He almost laughed at the name.

He made mental notes as he continued monitoring the asteroid as it slowly tumbled. He knew Murphy would order a boarding party soon, likely when she returned to the Bridge. He shook his head slowly. He didn't dislike Murphy, but she certainly wasn't his favorite on board. But captains didn't need to be popular, just good at what they did. Murphy was good at her job, if a bit immature. Being ten years her senior, though, made it easy for Gil to say.

His post at Tactical was his idea of perfection in Earthfleet, though he'd not advanced in rank in over five years. He knew eventually he would, and they'd all be transferred to other assignments, all larger ships. Because there were no smaller ships in Earthfleet that actually carried out deep-space missions.

Of course, that was assuming they all lived through the coming year on board *Pheidippides*. And survived whatever this thing they'd found really was.

* * *

"Duty Log, Lieutenant Commander Jennifer Murphy, 121017.15. After two days of monitoring with no additional EMP's or other interference, I've decided to send a boarding team to the object… ship, whatever you want to call it.

"This thing is huge. General characteristics show it's basically a big box, about two hundred fifty meters long, a hundred meters at the widest point, about the same depth, and has two very early style hyperlight engines tacked on. One is obviously dead, with a ten-meter hole through the phase coil units and a shattered hydrogen collector. Something obviously hit it hard a long time ago. The other one is simply nonfunctional, and one of the things we'll try to learn is why. And if this thing really is over two hundred years old, how did it get all the way out here on the edge of neutral space?

With a boarding team of four, we'll be short-handed on the ship, so everyone is at stations and running on caffeine and stims. Including me."

* * *

EAS Pheidippides…

The skiff was both shuttle and lifeboat for *Pheidippides*. Technically, it could accommodate a maximum of eight crew members, ten if the environmental systems were extended and all other electronics on board were minimized. Apparently, Earthfleet's thinking was, if the skiff was needed as a shuttle, no more than eight would be necessary during a mission, and if it was used as a lifeboat, no more than ten would have survived whatever calamity befell the ship.

Early in her command, Murphy had ordered modifications to the tiny craft, providing two temporary bunks for off-duty personnel and additional oxygen supplies and changes to the electrical feeds. Taylor Thomas and his E-techs had done a fine job of working up ways for the entire fourteen-person crew of *Pheidippides* to debark, if necessary. Regardless Murphy's perceived personality defects, she would never allow herself to leave crew behind if there was any way to avoid it.

"Captain, may I speak with you?" Jia-Lan Wèi stood at the side of Murphy's command seat.

Murphy gave her a look. "I know your question, and the answer is—"

"Captain, I've accepted the doctor's advice regarding not leaving the ship after my first trimester, but this may be my only chance for a landing party of any kind. I know I'm only an ensign and graduated barely a year ago, but my marks on Tactical and Comm systems are good. I can identify unusual patterns in signals and have cracked every test on encryption I've ever been given. I deserve a seat on the boarding party excursion." Wèi stood stiffly, waiting for Murphy's response.

Murphy counted to ten before she spoke. "You should make a mental note, Ensign, to not interrupt your captain when she's talking."

Wèi's face flushed. "Sorry, I was just…"

"My answer is, I approved your seat when talking with Lieutenant Ch'rehrin. He agreed, you would be an asset to the team."

Wèi blinked twice, then relaxed. "Geez, I'm sorry, Murphy… I mean, Captain. I've never done anything like that."

"See you don't do it again. Your next commanding officer might not be so forgiving." Murphy showed a slight grin. "Go knock 'em dead, Girl."

Wèi straightened, beamed a smile in return, and headed for the exit. Murphy only shook her head.

"Captain, I have additional information." Ch'rehrin stepped from his station to Murphy's side. "There is only a single hatchway on the object, very well hidden in the sublight drive section. There are no lifeboats behind the hatches, no auxiliary craft in the hangar, and no life readings we can determine. There appears to be no crew aboard, and the ship fully automated."

Murphy breathed a sigh of relief. "Still doesn't preclude finding bodies, and I hope that's not the case. While this simplifies things, it raises a lot more questions."

Ch'rehrin continued. "It also complicates our entry. There is only one docking port and it matches no current Earthfleet configuration, therefore crossing to the vessel must be done in EVA suits. As we have only four on board, I recommend we take two."

Murphy shook her head. "That will take twice the time for you to do your investigation. Take all four. Let's get this done quickly as possible. Besides, if you have only two suits, and transfer back and forth, in an emergency, you might have to leave someone behind. I don't find that acceptable."

Ch'rehrin considered, then nodded. "However, should we need to be rescued, it would likely prove impossible to do so."

Now Murphy mused the point. "Take three suits. Leave one of your team on the skiff at all times. Compromise."

"We will rotate the boarding party as needed. Very well, Captain." He turned back to his board as Murphy looked around the Bridge.

All stations were manned, the screen showed the vessel in the distance, however difficult it was to see directly, but Tactical had put a target ring on the image, to follow the object's orbit about the asteroid. Murphy watched absently for a few minutes. *What is this thing? How did it get here? And what can we do with it... if anything?*

* * *

The Boarding Party...

"Approaching at ten KPS relative," reported Lieutenant Ball at the skiff controls. "All nonessential electronics are shut down."

"Very good." Ch'rehrin looked to Jia-Lan Wèi and Hatu Gil in the seats behind him, already in their EVA suits. His was fully ready, but he had not yet donned his helmet. "Mr. Ball, you will remain on board, and once we have accessed the hatch, please take the skiff to a parking orbit, ten kilometers distant. Keep the hatch in sight at all times and maintain constant communications with me and the Tactical station on *Pheidippides*."

"Yes, sir. Just a reminder, your suits are good for four hours, with a thirty-minute reserve. And don't forget to leave breadcrumbs."

Ch'rehrin turned to Ball for a moment, then nodded. "Thank you for the reminder."

"I'm in charge of the breadcrumbs," said Wèi with a grin. "Today we have sourdough."

A quiet laugh passed between the humans. Ch'rehrin showed a wan smile.

"Coming up on the hatch. Geez, look at the size of this thing." Ball whistled.

"It's basically a very large container," said Gil, "but not as massive as I thought for something so big." He peered out a port. "Whatever hit the starboard engine took out half the fuel feed lines and most of the coolant system, which probably shut down the reactors. That's why it's still in one piece. Relatively speaking."

"Sir, I see markings," said Wèi. She stood, looking out the port opposite Gil. "Only partial, as most of it is still covered by the reflective panels." She sat and looked to Ch'rehrin. "One of the first things we should try to locate is how to turn those things off."

"Not necessarily, Ensign," replied the Arnec. "Should we do that, and other ships have followed, they would locate the vessel much more easily."

"You have to admit," said Ball, easing back on the thrusters, "it's low-tech, but very effective. No power required, other than to uncover the panels, then everything switches off. Like opening or closing a window shade." He pressed the thruster switches and sat back. "We're here, sir. Five hundred meters of empty space between us and the hatch."

Ch'rehrin looked to Gil and Wèi. "We will stay linked at all times during the transit. I have a safety line attached to the skiff anchor point with a magnetic release. Crossing will be done at ten second intervals."

"Aye, sir," chorused Gil and Wèi. They lowered their faceplates as Ch'rehrin donned his helmet.

"Green," said Gil, checking his suit tell-tales.

"Green," repeated Wèi. She closed her eyes and took a deep breath.

"Green also." Ch'rehrin nodded to the small airlock at the rear of the skiff. "Ms. Wèi… after you."

* * *

The hatch had no lock, other than a triple-redundant latching system. Ch'rehrin had anticipated it might be welded or bolted shut, but it turned out not to be the case. Entry was straight-forward and took only a few minutes to insure they would not be locked in, once they entered and the hatch closed again. They tried it three times before proceeding.

The airlock was large enough for all three of them, but not by much. "Anything larger than people must have gone through the docking port," said Wèi. "This is probably the auxiliary or emergency exit."

"*Good guess,*" said Ball from the skiff. "*This thing looks like the biggest cargo container I've ever seen.*"

"Dark, sir," said Gil, taking point, as they went through the inner hatch.

The light from their helmet lamps revealed narrow passageways, only wide enough for a single person. Gil's hand scanner cast colored lights about. "No air, no lights, no heat or environmental systems of any sort in this area." He glanced at his chronometer tell-tale. "Three hours and a bit left before we hit our reserve."

"Proceed quickly, as we need to find a control nexus, if one exists," replied Ch'rehrin.

"There has to be a main control room," said Wèi. "If this thing really was built for non-occupancy, even if there isn't a Bridge, there's got to be a main board."

"Lieutenant Gil, go to infrared on your detectors. Look for heat sources or simple variations in temperature as we proceed."

"Yes, sir." Gil anchored his hand-held on his chest plate and reset his wrist controls.

"These walls are thin, no more than four inches or so," said Wèi, probing with her scanner as they made their way slowly in the corridor.

"I track you as fifty meters beyond the hatch," came Ball's voice again. *"No real interference at all. Whatever the walls are, they're pretty inert."*

"Carbon fiber composites," replied Ch'rehrin, scanning as well. "Excellent strength, yet low mass." He aimed his scanner toward a wall, then paused. "Structural elements at ten-meter intervals, also carbon fiber construction."

"They built to last," said Wèi.

"Lieutenant Ch'rehrin, I'm detecting a widening of the passage ahead, and doors." Gil paused, and the trio came to a stop. "We're about a third of the way into the vessel."

"Proceed slowly to the doors, do not open or activate them until we have a chance to examine," said Ch'rehrin.

Twenty paces more brought them to a double set of entries, manually operated, with simple handles and double magnetic locks. Gil tried one, but it didn't move. He put serious muscle into another attempt, but the lock held. He backed away and consulted his scanner. "Basic construction again, but these magnets are pretty powerful. There has to be a bit of power to keep them activated."

Wèi knelt with her helmet light illuminating a panel on the door. "We'll never move this without cutting the power. The room beyond appears to be shielded, and this door is durasteel." She moved aside and aimed her scanner to the wall. "Here, too. Looks like the walls back at least ten meters are durasteel."

Ch'rehrin considered for a moment. "I'll contact the ship and ask the captain for instructions. Lieutenant Ball, patch me through to *Pheidippides.*"

Ball chuckled in the intercom. "*You're already on, sir. The whole ship is listening, I'll bet.*"

* * *

EAS Pheidippides…

Murphy sat in the command seat, watching the screen and listening to the running commentary between the boarding party, the skiff, and Tactical, where Lieutenant Demarcy and Martin Teng-Hey worked to keep the comm line and threat assessment issues clear. Between the concern about another EMP occurrence, interference of some sort within the vessel, and general nervousness throughout the mission, she found it a wonder the tension level on the Bridge wasn't higher.

On the other hand, she thought wryly to herself, *maybe I'm not such a bad captain after all. It's obviously my calm and reserved demeanor.*

For the better part of the A-shift she'd been considering what to do about the object, should they find its purpose. It was obviously of Earth origin, likely early Earthfleet, and therefore, government property. However, it had been missing, presumed destroyed or lost or maybe just forgotten about, for over two hundred years. Did that make it salvage? Did deep space prospector or treasure hunter laws apply?

If the thing was no longer in Earthfleet records, how did the OC orders lead us to it? Recent analysis? Old data resurfacing in computers? Wild-ass guess? Murphy didn't know.

What ticked at the back of her mind was, with the proximity to Qoearc space, what would the High Command offer for such an item?

Being Qoearc, of course, they'd favor weapons, defenses, superior or unique propulsion systems, or similar technology having a wartime application. A two hundred-year-old derelict likely possessed none of these things. Other races? Unlikely. According to their star maps, the Qoearc had subjugated everything and everyone within ten light years, maybe more. Next question.

How had it gotten out here? The old-style engines would have taken years, decades, to make the journey. But it had been many decades. And the current path showed the object wouldn't intersect the border at all, and was, in fact, on a somewhat lengthy voyage, as in centuries, toward neutral space. Which technically, they were in, but still…

What to do, what to do…

"Captain, Lieutenant Ch'rehrin is asking for you." Teng-Hey's voice broke Murphy's ruminations.

"On my comm, Martin."

The speaker crackled slightly. *"Ch'rehrin here, Captain. We have reached an area that appears to be shielded and cannot be accessed."*

"A locked room, hey?" Murphy nodded. "Not entirely unexpected, was it? What's on the other side?"

A pause. *"We're not sure, Captain,"* came Wèi's voice. *"But Lieutenant Gil says it doesn't appear to be a security issue, just structural. The area is roughly circular and three or four decks tall. The entire thing could be a module, dropped into the center of the ship."*

"If it's just a module, why is the thing so big?" asked Murphy.

"Unknown, Captain," replied Ch'rehrin. *"We've been aboard less than two hours, and this is our first indication of anything other than corridors and passages of relatively light, non-load-bearing construction. We may find differences elsewhere."*

"Can you get through the passages? Make a shortcut around the module?"

"Gil here, Captain. Yes, our torches on low power can easily cut through the walls without residual harm. We can do it cleanly."

"Is the skiff on the line?"

"Ball here, Captain."

"What are your sensors telling you, Lieutenant?"

There was a pause as they waited for him to read the data. *"Now that I know where to look, this area seems to be about a hundred meters in diameter and fifty or sixty thick. It's all shielded, so this is likely the control center, or power grid, or both. It's durasteel, and I doubt hand torches could get through it."*

"What about locks?" asked Murphy, thinking quickly.

"Electro-magnetic, and too strong to force, Captain," replied Ch'rehrin.

"Cheater bar."

Gil spoke off the comm, then back into the pickup. *"If we had one, it might work, but these passages are clear, Captain."*

"What if we cut the latch itself?" asked Wèi. Again, there was a pause. *"The latch and door plate are mild steel, Captain. I think we can get through."*

"I feel like a burglar," mumbled Murphy.

"Captain?"

"Nothing, Mr. Ch'rehrin, just thinking out loud. Alright, since you're two hours in, return to the skiff, take a rest, and let us think about this. Take whatever readings you can on the door, the latch, the plate, and let's talk this over before we go breaking and entering. For all we know, there may be monsters on the other side."

Gil chuckled, as did Wèi and Ball.

"That," said Ch'rehrin, completely deadpan, *"would be highly unlikely. For one thing, what would they have eaten for two hundred years?"*

"Hell, I don't know, maybe they rationed out the crew." Murphy paused, waiting for an acerbic reply from the Arnec, but none came. "Return to the skiff and let's review our options. We need to find out what's on the other side of that door, but we're going to do this like Earthfleet officers, not bandits."

Three
Bounty

"Duty Log, Lieutenant Commander Jennifer Murphy, 121217.14. We held a comm debriefing with the boarding party, now I've ordered six hours rest, a sonic shower, and a meal for all of them. It's tough enough off-ship, but even worse when you can't keep yourself clean or you're hungry and tired.

"In the meantime, the ship is running smoothly, but everyone is a bit stressed, standing nearly double watches and constantly on alert. Tactical keeps picking up flashes as though something is still out there, just at the edge of detection. Diagnostics show everything is working, so it's not ghosts in the machine. We'll keep our eyes sharp and prepare for whatever comes. This is beginning to feel like a lengthy mission, not to mention a critical one."

* * *

Six hours on the Bridge, and after conferences with the landing party, Engineering, and the Tactical group, Murphy ordered seconds to critical posts. She visited Engineering briefly, confirmed with Thomas that ship's functions were nominal, then walked slowly to the mess.

It came to her then… She pressed her wrist comm button with a shaking hand. "Comm, Murphy. Did we ever send an acknowledgement to Fleet after receiving our OC squirt?"

"Honley here, Captain. Let me take a quick look."

Murphy laid her back against the wall and closed her eyes, waiting. She couldn't understand the thoughts running through her mind.

"Captain, I show no messages from Fleet except the orders received when we were on the planet, followed days later by the OC squirt. Neither was acknowledged from our side. Shall I send a reply?"

Murphy took a deep breath. "No. Since this is an OC mission, we can't compromise our location. Until we have something important to report, we'll keep radio silence."

"Aye, Captain. Anything else?"

"Just keep your ears open for anything beyond our vicinity. There still may be Qoearc lurking in the distance."

"Will do."

Murphy clicked off and thumped the back of her head against the wall. *I need a drink.*

* * *

Murphy bypassed the mess, headed for Sickbay.

"Can I help you, Captain?" Nurse Butler was at the desk, and stood as Murphy entered.

"Is Doc off duty?"

"Yes, she's in the lab, left here about a half hour ago."

Murphy nodded thanks and nearly sprinted around the tight curve of the corridor. She found Melinkov at a small computer station, reading.

"Good day, Captain. Tea?"

Murphy slid a chair over and accepted the cup gratefully. She drank, draining nearly every drop. The doctor refilled it, watching her carefully.

"Something is on your mind, Captain."

It was not a question, and Murphy nodded. "I'm contemplating a life-changing event and need someone to talk me out of it."

"Truly? How so?"

Murphy drank again, then stared into her empty cup. "Do you know the word 'treasure-hunter', Doctor?"

Melinkov considered. "I understand the concept, however in Russian language, there are many variations, as there are in English."

"Such as?"

Melinkov shrugged. "For one, 'bounty hunter', or perhaps 'glory-seeker'. The phrase may be considered in several ways, Captain. However, I do not think you are looking for this answer, yes?"

Murphy shook her head, pausing. "I'm not sure what I'm looking for. As I said—"

"Yes, I heard you well. You are contemplating a course of action you do not wish to take, but may be forced to. Correct?"

"Not… exactly."

Melinkov sipped her tea. "Mm… then what, Captain?"

Murphy closed her eyes, saying nothing.

"Why did you join Earthfleet?"

Murphy looked at Melinkov from beneath her lowered brow. "I didn't have many choices."

"You were an excellent student in medical school until you, shall we say, lost your way."

"My mother died. I… fell apart. I flunked out in a single semester. I bummed around San Francisco for a year before I enlisted. Got pushed back toward med school and said no thanks. Then was offered a scholarship on athletics and screwed that up, too."

"Yet you finished your schooling and graduated near the top of your class."

"Yeah. Now I owe Earthfleet for the remainder of my education, about two years' worth. They take it out of my pay, did you know that, too?"

"No, but I have heard of similar situations." Melinkov refilled both cups and drank again. "So, what is this thing I am to talk you out of, Captain? Can it be so serious that you need your doctor's advice?"

Murphy grunted. "Touché." They laughed together, then were silent for a moment. "What would you think about a change of career, Doc?"

Melinkov shrugged. "I have often thought a life of beach-combing would be wonderful. However, I do not care for the beach, nor many of the lifeforms inhabiting the oceans. Therefore, I would simply sit in my dacha, drink tea, and read. I might do that in the middle of the city, no? Where there are many more other distractions as well."

"Ever thought about being a treasure-hunter? And coming upon the greatest treasure you could ever imagine?"

Melinkov studied Murphy's face. "I think there is another word more appropriate here, Captain."

"I figured you would. And that word would be…?"

"In Russian, it is pronounced something like '*yerapt*'. It is a simple word with a simple meaning."

"*Yerapt,*" Murphy repeated. "And its meaning?"

Melinkov drank and set down her cup, meeting Murphy eye to eye. "Pirate."

Murphy held her breath, then relaxed a bit. "You know me too well, Doc."

"I also know you are a good officer and not stupid. I know you have issues with authority, but desire structure in your life. I know you are strong in many ways, and one of those ways is in knowing when to do the right thing."

"And this is one of those times, right?"

Melinkov shrugged again. "I cannot say for you. I can only advise what I observe."

"I think you've already made pretty clear, Doc."

She nodded. "Then you have only to consider your own actions, which affect many people besides yourself. After all, you are captain of this vessel, and the crew looks to you for guidance."

"Laying it on pretty thick, aren't you, Doc?"

"As you say. However, as you consider this change of careers, as you call it, also consider the consequences. Where would you go? Whom could you trust? Could you live always looking over your shoulder, knowing you had betrayed vows and friends and family?"

"You sound like a holo-movie."

Melinkov nodded, side to side. "Perhaps I have watched too many old stories. Think also, we have been out here nearly a year with no contact other than ourselves. You now have a new life coming into the world under your command. You have found a great prize, a treasure as you say, that does not belong to you, or may belong to no one, depending on whom you ask. What will you do? Only you can say, and I do not think you have that answer yet."

Murphy was silent for a time. "The question in my mind is, what will you do, Doc?"

Melinkov shrugged with her eyes. "Concerning what? We are only talking, yes, to fill the time? One must let one's mind play out scenarios when necessary, to make the right choice. We have spoken on occasion, and I knew at some point in our mission, you would come to me with concerns. This has been building for a time, Captain, and only now do you have an opportunity worth true consideration. I would hope you do so with all factors in mind."

* * *

The Boarding Party…

Ch'rehrin sat away from the other crew, contemplating. That is, if one could truly "sit away" in a craft as small as the skiff, it was what he chose to do. Between Ball's gentle snoring as he slept, Wèi flipping pages back and forth in her report folder, to the incessant rattle of the air system blower, the need for solitude pressed in on him. If he could not be alone physically, mentally would have to do.

The Arneci were a passionate people, but had learned the hard way that passions could be the way to destruction. They shared much in common with humans, in that war had plagued their world for centuries. It was only when they came to the realization that there could be only one ending, things began to change. That, too, had taken centuries. And lives. Many, many lives.

Humans were the first alien species the Arneci had encountered in their stellar travels, and they, in turn, were the first for humans as well. It had been a fortuitous meeting, in many ways, and the cooperation had grown quickly. Now, with Arneci serving on many Earthfleet ships, and human scientists aiding in researching issues of genetic problems and mutations in the Arneci population, the paring of the two Races became more than its parts. Mutual dependence took the place of mutually assured destruction. And friendships had grown, in and out of Earthfleet and the Earth Alliance.

Ch'rehrin smiled softly at the remembrances. And the opportunities, as this one, such cooperation had afforded him and many of his kind.

The mystery of the vessel was his most interesting concern, but with that was the uniqueness of the mission itself. Never, in his fifteen-year Earthfleet career, had he seen an OC issue occur, nor the need for, as humans said, a "cover story" of the Qoearc mining project. Further, assignment of such a covert task to *Pheidippides,* and its somewhat ill-suited commanding officer, seemed, to be blunt, ill-advised. Yet, as they were the only Fleet ship in the area, and the arrival of any substantial forces would draw notice by the Qoearc, likely this was the best course of action… for the moment.

Ch'rehrin knew they had a very limited time to learn whatever secrets this discovery held. He reasoned at least one Qoearc ship was watching nearby, just out of detection range. There might be drones hovering around, too small or too stealthed to be noticed by even *Pheidippides's* sensors. He made a mental note to recommend Murphy send one of theirs on a scouting mission of its own.

He glanced at the chronometer. He would wait one more hour, then wake Ball, leave Wèi in the skiff for this foray, and attempt entry into the fortified area of the vessel. Whatever was in there, and it had to be a substantial volume of something, was apparently important enough for whoever launched it to protect.

Like most Arneci, he did not speculate; rather; he would work through progressions and possibilities of what the contents might be. But at this moment, and to his chagrin, he could find no answer to the situation.

Perhaps that was why humans were better guessers and tacticians than Arneci. Because of their illogic.

* * *

EAS Pheidippides…

Murphy closed and sealed the door to her quarters. She sat on her bunk, numb to the core. The doctor had seen right through her, as she usually did. Just like her mom had done, every single time Murphy tried something stupid. Or dangerous. Or really, really interesting.

Okay, now what? Nothing, I guess. I'm an Earthfleet officer and I have a job to do. If I don't do it, then what? I'm out of the service? Brought up on charges? Mutinied against? An "unfortunate accident where the captain tried to do something she shouldn't have"? Get a posthumous citation for "bravery"? Cripes, how stupid could I be?

She swore beneath her breath.

I'm less than a year from getting off this ship, maybe sooner if we come back with a real treasure for Fleet to pat us on the back for. On the other hand, if we do such a good job, they may just send us right back out again. No good deed goes unpunished, right? She shook her head at her own joke.

The intercom squawked. *"Captain, Bridge. Lieutenant Ch'rehrin is on the horn and is asking for the Captain's recommendations."* Honley's voice was far too cheerful for Murphy's mood.

She hit the intercom switch a bit too hard. "Ten minutes, Chuck. I'm in the Head seeing a dog about a man."

Honley made a desperate attempt to suppress his laughter. He clicked off without acknowledging.

Murphy took moments to wash her face, change jumpsuit, and shake her hair out, then tie it back again. *Maybe I tied it too tight earlier and that made my brain screwy. Sure… any excuse for admitting to the doctor you wanna be a pirate when you grow up.*

She sighed and walked out the door, taking the few steps needed to enter the Bridge.

* * *

The Boarding Party…

Ch'rehrin waited with Gil and Ball by the durasteel doors at the shielded area entrance. They had confirmed the latch plate and handle were mild steel, a design error none of them could explain. Regardless, it was their only option to enter the shielded area and see what lay within.

"Murphy here. You're at the doors, Lieutenant?"

"Affirmative, Captain, waiting for instructions."

"Permission to cut the latch plate. Be gentle with it. Don't want to wake the monsters."

Ch'rehrin nodded to Gil, then he and Ball stepped back ten paces. Gil set his torch for low power and aimed at a corner of the plate and pressed the trigger. The steel cut, but slowly.

"Going to medium power," said Gil, then aimed again. This time, the crimson beam burned easily through the target, and in less than a minute, the latch plate and lever floated free.

"Don't touch it," said Ball.

Gil only nodded. The metal was obviously hot, and emitted a drifting cloud of particles. They tracked it as it cooled, then Ball plucked it out of the passage vacuum and stuffed it into his carry-all.

"Captain, we've removed the latch and plate." Ch'rehrin motioned Gil to play his light through the opening to see what he might.

"Dark, but a lot of… looks like tanks. Or vats. Hard to tell, but the area is full of them."

"Control boards, consoles, lights of any sort?" asked Wèi from the skiff.

"I suggest we enter, since we now have access," said Ch'rehrin.

"Proceed," replied Murphy. *"With caution."*

Gil swung the door open easily, then took a step inside. Overhead lights came on, soft, and leaving little room for shadows. A flicker, and slowly, they began to hear, through their external suit pickups, fans moving in the ceiling.

"Air pressure coming up, oxy-nitrogen mix." Ball reported as he watched his helmet tell-tales rise. "Should be breathable in a few minutes."

"Close the door and cover the hole made by our entry," ordered Ch'rehrin.

"Keep your suits sealed," came Murphy's voice from Pheidippides. *"Under no circumstances will you remove your helmets."*

"Understood, Captain." Ch'rehrin swept his eyes about, as did Gil and Ball.

They moved away from the door slowly, side arms in hand, looking round at the collection of tanks taking up most of the floor space. Each was about fifteen feet in diameter and five feet high, all durasteel. PADDs, or something like them, were mounted on the top center of each tank, with a continuous string of symbols running. Each tank was labeled in heavy black letters, all English language, obviously coded.

"Captain, what we're seeing—"

"I have the feed from your helmetcam, Mr. Ch'rehrin. Sweep the room slowly, then move to each tank individually and focus on the screen at the top of each one for ten seconds. Hatu, check

temp on these tanks if you can, Mr. Ball, look for the main panel and any access to the areas above."

"Wèi here, Captain. The energy output has gone up drastically from the vessel, but it's all centered in the area of the boarding party. Looks like the power source is one floor below. There must be some heavy shielding to keep us from detecting it previously."

"Thanks, Jia-Lan. Ch'rehrin, continue your sweep, Hatu, see if you can access the area below where you are. Don't descend, just find it."

"Captain, the main panel is on the wall ninety degrees from our entry point," said Ball. "It appears to be a feed from each of the tank screens, plus a lot of additional data, mostly environmental and engineering."

"Sounds about right," said Wèi, from the skiff.

"Captain, I can't tell anything about temperature in the tanks, but I get the impression whatever is in there is very cold. There are two vents on each tank and piping running down through the floor. Some of the vents are... well, venting, very slightly."

"Alright Hatu, don't worry about it. Look for access to the power source. Mr. Ch'rehrin, anything else?"

"Confirming Lieutenant Ball's findings, Captain. The main panel is a monitoring nexus for the tanks, and presumably the rest of the ship. There are forty tanks with heavily sealed and toggled lids. There is an apparatus at the ceiling with cables, pulleys, rigid connectors, and a large hook attachment to move over the tanks and lift the lids if necessary."

"Just say it's an overhead crane, Ch'rehrin."

"It is an overhead crane, Captain."

"Thank you."

Ball and Gil both snickered, and they thought they could hear Wèi nearly choking on her laughter.

* * *

EAS Pheidippides…

The intercom was quiet for a few minutes. Murphy looked around the Bridge. No one was actually laughing, but it was close. Honley at Comm had his face in both hands, away from Murphy. She shook her head, then hid her own grin.

"Chuck, send Lieutenant Ch'rehrin's camera feed to Doctor Melinkov's office." Murphy pressed the intercom button. "Sickbay, Bridge. Doc, take a look at these files and let me know what you think. Come to the Bridge when you've had a few minutes to review them." She clicked off. "Mr. Ch'rehrin, what's your time allowance?"

"We are well equipped, Captain, only now into our second hour of consumables. Your orders?"

Murphy dithered. "I want to discuss this with Doctor Melinkov before we proceed. In the meantime, continue searching for access above and below the level you're on. Once you find them, take five."

"I've found the hatch leading below, Captain," said Gil. *"And there are three ladders leading upward from various areas, all situated around the walls."* He swept his helmetcam slowly about.

"Good work, Hatu. OK, take a break, continue monitoring, and yell if anything pops up."

"Very well, Captain. Reports in fifteen-minute intervals until you give us new instructions." Ch'rehrin switched off the camera feed, but kept his comm line open.

"No change in energy output since the spike, Captain," reported Wèi in the skiff. *"Minor power sources above the level of our party."*

"Noted, Ensign. Keep your eyes on our crew."

An hour passed. Ch'rehrin checked in three times with new details, none of which were urgent. Murphy was about to order the boarding party back to the skiff when her intra-ship intercom light glowed. *"Bridge, this is Doctor Melinkov. Captain, will you join me in my office, please?"*

Murphy pressed the in-ship switch. "What have you got, Doc?"

"A possible answer to why this mission was OC priority. And maybe even an answer to what the vessel we are investigating might be."

Everyone on the Bridge turned to Murphy, nearly as one.

"On my way." She nearly ran to the doors.

* * *

It took Murphy less than thirty seconds to round the curve to Sickbay. Nurse Butler pointed to the office as she entered. Murphy closed the door behind her, then sat, nearly breathless.

Melinkov turned from her screen and folded her hands on the desk. "We have wondered why such a mission, a simple set of coordinates, was sent with such high priority, yes?"

"Your penchant for understatement is amusing sometimes, Doc, and for you to come up with this in a matter of an hour is pretty interesting."

"Can we speak with the First Officer on a private line?"

Murphy blinked. "Sure, but first, tell me why."

Melinkov sat back, regarding the captain. "I must first trust you again, Captain. Regarding our last conversation, I am… worried of your state of mind."

For a long moment, it wa silent in the tiny office. At last, Murphy waved a hand. "No longer an issue. I had a talk with myself and considered your advice. I decided to take it."

"Excellent, Captain. How do I know this as true?"

"Because… dammit, because what you said made me really consider what I want."

"And that is?"

Murphy looked away, saying nothing, then met Melinkov's eyes again. "I what to do what's right. For you, for the crew, for Earthfleet… but mostly for myself. I'm not a pirate. I'm just a bored officer looking for a thrill, and the type of Earthfleet I signed up for."

Melinkov held her gaze for a long time, then turned to the teapot in the corner and poured two cups. She set them on the desk, offered milk and sugar, then drank as Murphy stared blankly into hers.

"Earthfleet gave me a second chance after my fiasco in med school," said Murphy quietly. "I thumbed my nose at them with refusal to go back into medicine, then they gave me a third chance with the athletic scholarship. I screwed up again with my antics that got me tossed off the team, then they *still* gave me another chance with my education and the posting to this ship."

She drank before continuing. "Somebody saw something in me that I refused to see in myself. Maybe I still don't understand completely, and maybe I'm still looking for excuses, but I owe someone big time. If I screw this up, I'm done. Even if Fleet came back and said, 'give it another try', I could never look them in the face again. Or the crew. Or you." She swallowed hard, drained the cup, and looked away, obviously holding back her emotions.

"Your mother was very important in your life. You lost her when you were becoming a young woman, yet not knowing what to do with that womanhood." The doctor sipped. "In Russia, we grow faster, emotionally. We are forced to take more responsibility early in our lives, especially the girls. They become their mothers' extra hands, because even in this, how is it said, 'enlightened' age, tradition is hard to break in some places."

Murphy shrugged. "Maybe that's my problem. I should have been born in Russia."

Melinkov nodded. "Certainly, you would not have been so… what is the word? Coddled? Yes, coddled."

"Thanks, Doc."

"Is it not true?"

Murphy said nothing.

"Let us assume, for the moment, you are truthful, and once again the Earthfleet captain everyone wants you to be. How do we proceed?"

"You asked for a private line to my first officer. If I say yes, I want to be in the loop."

Melinkov nodded. "Of course, as you are the captain. I would not do so otherwise."

"Good. Now that the psyche exam is over, what's this all about?"

"Life, Captain. And escape from a world gone mad."

* * *

Melinkov had Murphy's full and undivided attention as she spoke. For nearly thirty minutes, the doctor outlined her theories, seemingly plucked from Wèi's data feeds, an hour's study of jumpy videos from Ch'rehrin's helmetcams, and thin air. Murphy asked no questions, made no gestures, no remarks, not so much as a wisecrack.

At last she let go a heavy breath. "Let's do this from here, in private. I don't want anyone to hear this but us, so we all have plausible deniability." She sat back, her nervousness slowly fading. "Doc, where do you come up with this stuff?"

"Clues. A treasure map, I believe you alluded to once, yes? Certainly, we have found a treasure, have we not?"

Murphy touched the intercom switch on the desk. "Comm, Sickbay. Chuck, set up a private line between this comm station and Lieutenant Ch'rehrin. Full encryption, full scramble, totally secure. And I mean totally, Chuck."

A pause. "*Aye, Captain. This has to go into the log, you know.*"

"Understood. But this is part of the OC matter, so it's 'eyes-only' on my authority. Log as necessary."

"*Yes, Captain.*" Honley was all business. "*Give me a few minutes and I'll call back.*"

Murphy clicked off and blew another breath. "OK, Doc, once this is on the record, then what.?"

Melinkov thought for a moment. "Then my work is done, and you will decide. Surely Earthfleet must be notified immediately if my suppositions are correct."

Murphy nodded. "Yeah… let's just hope no uninvited company shows up."

* * *

Ch'rehrin was studying the control board nexus when the call came to him. A tone sounded in his ear, then a second.

"This is a recording. The commanding officer of EAS Pheidippides has ordered a secure, private connection to your comm system. This communique is confidential to the highest order, and concerns an OC issue matter. Disclosure of this conversation to anyone other than the commanding officer of EAS Pheidippides or designated authority must be authorized by voice print, retinal scan, or other Earthfleet regulations. Disobeying of these orders is subject to review, reprimand, or court martial. This is the only warning you will receive regarding this matter. If you accept these conditions as an officer of Earthfleet, subject to all oaths given at the time of your enlistment and assignment, please say or type 'accepted'. You have ten seconds to comply, otherwise, this message will become null and void." Another tone sounded, then *"Ten seconds, mark."*

Ch'rehrin hesitated exactly three seconds. He was very careful with his voice as he said quietly, "Accepted."

He walked to a corner of the room away from Gil and Ball, talking quietly and sitting in fold-out chairs. His hands shook slightly as he waited, and he willed them calm, closed his eyes, and cleared his mind as he could. A tone sounded, then another. Then a third. He opened his eyes.

"Ch'rehrin here, awaiting connection."

Another tone. *"Lieutenant Eulenkav Ch'rehrin, this is Lieutenant Commander Jennifer Murphy and Doctor Ulyana Melinkov, speaking from the Sickbay office aboard EAS Pheidippides. Ship time is fourteen-thirty-two hours, Ship's Timemark 121517.10. Can you hear us clearly?"*

Ch'rehrin took a breath before answering. "I hear you clearly, Captain. My instruments show we have a private and secure connection. Please proceed."

"This is Doctor Melinkov. I have thoughts regarding the contents of the vessel you are currently investigating. I need to ask some questions of you, Lieutenant."

"Of course, Doctor."

"I have reviewed your visuals and comm data. The tanks appear to be cryogenic containers. The venting of gasses, the perceived cold reported by Lieutenant Gil, and the markings on the tank surfaces support this conclusion. It is important that we translate the codes as soon as possible. Is anyone in your party capable of doing this?"

Ch'rehrin's mind raced. Surely this was a job for someone in the encryption branch at Fleet Base Twenty-three! He took another breath. "The only member of our team with comm or encryption knowledge is Ensign Jia-Lan Wèi, currently on board the skiff in standard crew rotation, as discussed with the captain before we departed *Pheidippides*."

"Very well. Does the ensign have access to your visuals?"

"Yes, and has been studying them since our second foray began."

"Excellent. When this discussion is over, advise her it is imperative she decipher those markings as soon as possible. Further, I have theories I will now disclose to you."

"Before you begin, Doctor, please confirm you've discussed such theories with the captain, especially considering the sensitivity of this communication."

Melinkov's voice took on an even more formal tone. *"I assure you, I have done so. The captain and I have discussed these issues for nearly the last hour. It is by her order we are now talking with you."*

"Captain, please confirm."

"Confirmed, Lieutenant Ch'rehrin. This is the Big One."

Ch'rehrin paused. "Big One" was a phrase Murphy sometimes used when speaking of lofty goals, of finding the ultimate answers, or, as Arneci would say, "the sum of the universe". He shook his head slightly in disbelief. "Proceed, Doctor."

Melinkov continued. *"I have much research yet to do, but I believe we have found a myth, Lieutenant. There were stories in Russia many years ago when I was in medical school, of happenings after the Third War, the one nearly wiping out all of humanity. There were also tales from the wars that followed, but those have faded with the horrors from the Third War. Yet still they persist."*

"I have heard many of those stories myself, Doctor, but give little credence to them. But forgive my interruption and please continue."

Melinkov drew a breath on the intercom. *"There was a plan, say the tales, to save the world. Not the world of Earth, but the world of Humankind. To launch away from Earth an 'ark'. The tales say this 'ark' was never completed, never launched, and never more than a dream. Certainly, such a task would be difficult during the Third War. Yet stories persist it was a secret project done afterward, or perhaps before, depending on the source. What if it was hidden for that time, surviving everything that happened? There is evidence, though difficult to find, that says it may be so.*

"Still, it is said that once a thing is thought, it may be realized. I, myself, have seen such happen. Therefore, I lay this before you now, not as a myth, but a reality we could have never dreamed possible.

"It is my theory, Lieutenant, that within those cryogenic tanks you will find that world. Plants and animals of all varieties, in embryonic form. Seeds and egg cells and sperm from every species on Earth that was still viable during and after the Third War, and perhaps many before that time. Anything that could be

gathered, saved, and hidden away from those who sought to enslave not only humans, but all of the Earth itself.

Melinkov paused for effect. *"In one of those tanks you will find humans. Fertilized eggs, embryos of people yet to be born. Surely at least ten thousand. Perhaps as many as a million."*

"The 'Seeds of Eden'," breathed Ch'rehrin.

"Precisely. I see we are privy to the same stories, Lieutenant Ch'rehrin."

Four
Decisions

"Duty Log, Lieutenant Commander Jennifer Murphy, 121517.10. With the theories put forth by Dr. Melinkov, the focus of the boarding party has become deciphering of the codes seen on the tanks of the derelict vessel. I allowed Lieutenant Gil to remove one of his gloves and lay his bare hand onto a tank, which confirmed it was cold to the touch. Deep scanning has shown these tanks are heavily insulated, durasteel on the outside and some sort of honeycomb construction inside, with segmented areas. We presume each tank holds cells, spores, seeds, and other types of immature plants, animals, and yes, humans.

"General information regarding the derelict has been verbally disseminated, with strict orders not to discuss. I've allowed this for two specific reasons; crew efficiency, and the nipping in the bud the impossible task of keeping a secret on a ship this small.

"The hot topic on the ship's net is Svalbard Global Seed Vault, a depository created in the late nineteen-hundreds, old calendar. What we appear to have found is a later version of this, after the Svalbard location, and others like it throughout the world, were destroyed in the Third War.

"I cannot overstate the importance of this discovery. I also cannot imagine how Earthfleet lost track of it. But at the same time, if this was truly launched during or after the Third War, I salute the brave souls who sacrificed so much to make it possible, and see the dream succeed. I'm humbled that the crew of Pheidippides has the honor of retrieving such a treasure."

* * *

EAS Pheidippides…

"Captain, the skiff is docked and locked." Engineer Thomas's voice was filled with relief on the intercom.

Murphy pressed her command seat button. "Have them meet me in Sickbay immediately, Taylor. No detours."

"*Aye, Captain.*" Thomas switched off as Murphy pressed a second button. "Sickbay, Bridge. Doc, I'm on the way to you as are the skiff boarding party. Debriefing is priority one." Click.

"Ms. Connor, you have the conn, I'll be in conference. Maintain our position relative to the vessel, and keep your eyes peeled." Murphy headed out the door without waiting for a reply.

She met the boarding crew at the Sickbay door. "Before we enter, well done, all of you. I know it was tough and probably a bit scary, but really, an outstanding job. Thank you."

Gil, Ball, and Wèi grinned quietly in reply.

Ch'rehrin only nodded politely and gestured to the door. "Captain."

"Nurse Butler, since this is the only place aboard we can collect the necessary parties, please allow us some privacy. Take an hour off in your quarters or get a snack."

Butler glanced to the group before her, noting Murphy's "get out of here for a while" look. She nodded wordlessly, and took her exit quickly.

Melinkov emerged from her office in a clean, white smock. "You are to be commended, officers. This discovery is likely one of the most important in Earthfleet history. Allow me to offer my sincere congratulations and appreciation."

"I already gave them an official 'well done', Doc." Murphy grinned. "You don't have to show me up."

A small laugh went around the group.

Murphy paused, taking them all in with her eyes. "I know you're all beat, but we need to debrief quickly, while it's fresh. Yes, we've been in constant communication, and we have all the transcripts and notes, but I'm interested in your feelings about this thing."

Wèi spoke. "Captain, the markings on the tanks are as we suspected, codes for what's inside. They're pretty general, and I'm sure there's more information within the tanks. The data feeds contain plenty of information, though." She paused. "We're not thinking of digging into the tanks, are we?"

"That would not be advisable," said Melinkov, before Murphy could reply. "My professional opinion is they should not be disturbed in any fashion."

"Agreed, Doc," said Murphy. "Hatu, what about the power source?"

"Old-style nuclear, Captain, and from what I could tell, a thousand-year fuel source. It's pretty dirty, too."

"Dangerous?"

Gil shook his head. "Not unless it's breached. They built to last."

Murphy looked to Ball. "You checked out the levels above and found bunks?"

"Actually rooms, Captain, as shown in our vids. Thirty-four rooms total, sixteen singles and sixteen doubles. None of them have been used at all. Everything is pristine."

"So they launched without a crew. That tells me they were in a hurry or didn't have the crew assembled. Regardless, a pretty desperate move."

"Or one of simple precaution," said Ch'rehrin. "Without a crew, and unless programmed or given commands to return, the ship would stay on course. Obviously, the launching had to be done in secret, and in such a situation that no ships were available to track it and bring it back. Or destroy it."

Murphy nodded after a moment. "Point taken. Recommendations, Mr. Ch'rehrin, Doctor?"

"Continue the investigation, document findings thoroughly, and take all necessary precautions." Ch'rehrin nodded to Melinkov.

"Also prepare a preliminary report to Fleet Base Twenty-three, Captain, for dispatch as soon as possible."

Murphy pursed her lips. "With Qoearc lurking about, I'm reluctant to send any messages, Doc. OC regulations dictate radio silence until further contact by base."

"But in this case—"

"I understand your concern and don't disagree. But orders are orders, especially in a situation like this. Let's continue for twenty-four hours and see if we hear from Fleet." Murphy turned to Ch'rehrin. "Up for another foray? How about the rest of you?"

"We're prepared, Captain," replied Ch'rehrin. The others nodded eagerly.

"Alright, take six hours rest, use the sleep-sets if you need to. Okay with you, Doc?"

Melinkov nodded. "Food, a shower, clean coveralls. A bit of meditation would not be a bad thing, either."

Murphy motioned to the door. "You heard the doctor. Go say your mantra and burn your incense, but keep it quiet and in quarters. And no gossip." She looked to Wèi. "None."

* * *

Jia-Lan Wèi sat on the edge of her bunk. Her roommate, Karen Connor, was on the Bridge, so she had solitude and time to think, now that she had taken a quick shower and eaten a decent meal.

She twirled the sleep-set headpiece in her hand. The mission aboard the vessel had been exciting and a bit scary, as the captain had said, but also, now that she knew what was likely contained in the cryo-tanks, it had taken on a whole new meaning. This wasn't just a mission; this could be the future of Mankind. There were plenty of human colonies in and even beyond Earth Alliance Space, but this… this was a voice from the past, species and genera, and even breeds no longer existing on Earth. She'd always had a passing interest in biology, but this… event seemed to have raised it to a roaring fire.

Or maybe it was just her own pregnancy that made her more aware. She laid her hand on her belly gently. *Yeah, carrying a new life in your own body gives one a different view, that's for sure.*

The door chimed.

"Come in."

Martin entered quietly, and she rose to kiss him. They held each other for a moment, then Jia-Lan drew back and beamed. "It was amazing. Maybe you can get a seat on the next foray."

"Yeah… rumors are rampant about what's aboard."

"Martin, you know I can't talk about it. OC, and all that."

He looked away, nodding slightly.

"… What's wrong?"

He took a seat at the tiny desk under the hull curvature and shook his head, still not meeting her eyes.

"Look at me, mister." Jia-Lan grinned and laid a hand on his arm. He drew it away. Her face fell.

Martin blew a breath and shrugged. "I don't know… if I'm ready to be a father."

* * *

"Captain Murphy, Sickbay. Can you come to my office at your earliest convenience?" Doctor Melinkov's voice was coldly formal.

Murphy sat straighter in her command seat and pressed the intercom button. "Sure, Doc. What's up?"

"Private consultation."

Cripes. Murphy sighed. "On my way." She pressed the button again. "Karen, you have the conn. I'll be in Sickbay."

She exited and rounded the corridor curve, entered Sickbay and looked to the doctor's office.

"Here, Captain." Melinkov was at one of the three beds with Ensign Wèi, her eyes red and puffy.

Murphy approached, a disgusted look on her face. "I know that look."

Melinkov nodded. "This is a private matter, between Ensign Wèi and Lieutenant Teng-Hey, Captain. However, since it may affect crew morale and ship's operation, it was necessary to bring it to your attention."

"I… had a feeling. I'm sorry, Jia-Lan. I won't say what I really feel, but trust me, I understand your situation." Murphy paused, then lowered her voice. "He's a creep. But you can move on from this. You're strong, and brave, and young."

Wèi nodded listlessly.

"Still want to go on the next foray to the vessel?"

Jia-Lan looked up. "Of course, Captain. But—"

"What, you thought I was going to make you sit at your station and mope? Not a chance. You've got a job to do, so go do it. Feathers in your cap, and all that."

Jia-Lan showed a weak smile. "Aye, Captain. Don't want to disappoint all those admirals, right?"

Melinkov nodded, satisfaction in her face. "Very good, Captain. Ensign, I suggest you prepare for your next mission."

Jia-Lan rose, nodded to them, and left Sickbay.

"What of the Lieutenant?" asked Melinkov.

"What about him? He's not broken any laws or regs. Let him stew in his own decisions. His loss."

The doctor thought for a moment. "However…"

"As you said, Doc, it's between the two of them. Let them sort it out. We've got a job to do here. Once we're back at base, there will be plenty of time for whatever discussions they want to have."

"As you say, Captain. Still there is time."

"Captain Murphy, this is Ch'rehrin. We are preparing to debark, waiting now on Ensign Wèi."

Murphy pressed her wrist comm button. "She's on her way. Proceed at your discretion once she's on board. Report when you're at the vessel."

"Understood. Ch'rehrin out."

Murphy switched off and looked again to Melinkov. "Back to work, Doc. Can't keep all those admirals waiting."

* * *

The Boarding Party…

"Close to within one hundred meters this time, Lieutenant," said Ch'rehrin. "Then a parking station, five kilometers away."

"A bit closer, sir?" Gil nudged the controls. "No disagreement. Passing half a kilometer in open space was the longest half-hour I ever want to spend."

"Clear space," said Wèi from the Nav console. "Who's staying this time?"

"Rock, Paper, Scissors?" asked Ball with a grin. "You're on!" They swung around, facing each other after Gil locked the controls.

"Go!" Wèi slammed her hand flat onto her palm. "Damn!" She looked to Ch'rehrin. "Sorry, sir."

"You always go for paper," said Gil, showing scissors, as did Ball.

"Ensign, it appears you are the odd woman out," said Ch'rehrin, showing a hint of a smile. "Keep full comm with all of us and the ship, as before. Full recordings and vid augmentation as required."

"I know the drill, sir. Thank you for the reminder."

Ch'rehrin turned to the others. "Lieutenant Gil, continue your analysis of the power source. Mr. Ball, you have yet to access the top deck, correct?"

"Yes, sir, that's my first priority, above the crew quarters."

Ch'rehrin nodded. "Very well. Be judicious in your investigation." He closed his helmet visor.

"You okay, Jia-Lan?" Ball asked quietly. They stood as he suited up.

She nodded. "A bit tired, but yeah, I'm okay. Thanks for asking." She smiled softly at him.

The trio moved to the airlock and entered. Wèi took the command seat and activated the comm channel. "*Pheidippides*, this is Wèi on board the skiff. The boarding party is on the way to the vessel. Stand by for full link to the group comm."

* * *

EAS Pheidippides…

Murphy listened casually to the banter between Tactical, Nav, and the boarding party. Twice she spoke with Taylor Thomas in Engineering to assure herself the ship was ready for whatever might come, be it Qoearc, a rescue should it be necessary, or monsters from the vessel, as she and Ch'rehrin had joked about. She ordered a crew member into the fourth E-suit, stationed at the airlock, just in case. After an hour, she decided she was being selfish, and called the whole thing off. Right after which, Demarcy at Tactical shouted for attention.

"Captain, we have a bogey!"

Murphy came instantly alert. "Bearing, Lieutenant, distance, all the details now. Nav, what are you showing?"

"Indeterminate readings, Captain. Something is out there, but I don't know exactly where or what it is."

"Tactical?"

Demarcy shook his head and cursed under his breath. "Just… yeah, it's out there, but I can't find it now. It was a quick burst, neutrinos, like a power surge."

"Qoearc?"

"No idea, Captain. It's there, then it isn't. If it's stealthed, it's damn good."

Murphy turned to Martin at the Comm station. "Get me Ch'rehrin, pronto."

"He's on, Captain, private line."

"Lieutenant Ch'rehrin, we've got company."

The line was quiet for a moment. *"Acknowledged, Captain, what are your orders?"*

"Captain, it's coming in fast! Locked in, ten million kilometers and headed straight for us!"

No time to get back to the skiff, Murphy thought. "Gather your crew and find shelter, the best place you can get that will mask your suit signals and comm."

"That would likely be the power source level, Captain. What of the skiff?"

"Martin, put this signal through to the skiff." Murphy waited for the connection.

"Skiff here, Captain, Ensign Wèi."

"Jia-Lan, we have an unidentified ship incoming. I want you to look around as quickly as possible and see if there is a nook or cranny you can tuck the skiff into somewhere in the superstructure. Maybe even get it under some of those reflective panels that are loose."

"What about – "

"They've got to shelter in the vessel. No time. Do it now, but don't endanger yourself or the skiff. As soon as we have a vector, we'll let you know, and at least you can keep the vessel between you and the intruder."

"Aye, Captain. Pulling away from the parking orbit now, thrusters only."

"Good girl. Ch'rehrin, status?"

"We are making way into the power level, Captain. Two minutes."

"Captain, whatever this thing is, it's bigger than a scout!" Demarcy turned, and Murphy spun her finger for him to face his instruments. "It's swinging parallel to the Qoearc border, slowing…"

"Distance?"

"Five million kilometers, heavy stealthing, huge power output now!"

Murphy looked to O'Brien and Connor. "Battle Stations, prepare countermeasures. Confirm polarization and stand by to reverse, if necessary. Lock and load torpedo tube, PAKS at ready."

She nearly white-knuckled the arms of the command seat. *Big One, indeed.*

* * *

The Boarding Party…

Ch'rehrin followed Gil around what he recognized as an ancient reactor complex, nearly filling the entire lower deck of the vessel. Twice they doubled-back, and twice more they changed their hiding place, simply because there was not room for all three of them. At last they settled in a dark enclosure with a massive hatch, likely a safe room in case there had been a radiation accident during construction. The shielding was too heavy for their communicators to penetrate. Ch'rehrin considered how they might know when it was safe to emerge.

"We will stay here for a half hour, then one of us will check the comm channel outside this enclosure," he said.

"What about the skiff?" asked Ball.

"There is little we can do, Lieutenant. The captain ordered Ensign Wèi to hide the skiff if possible, or keep the vessel between it and the intruder."

"Intruder," repeated Gil. "Think it's the Qoearc shadowing us before?"

Ch'rehrin considered. "Based on what comm I received from the ship, very possible." He thought to say more, but refrained. He knew, if it came to fighting over the vessel,

Murphy might be forced to destroy it, lest it be captured by Qoearc… or others. He also knew *Pheidippides* was not, in any manner, a fighting ship. Likely the others of the boarding party realized this point, as well.

"Mark, thirty minutes," said Ball, clicking his chronometer. He looked around, settled in a corner, and turned off his helmet light.

"Keep conversation to a minimum," said Ch'rehrin.

Gil nodded, sat as well, and Ch'rehrin followed, turning down the intensity on his head lamp.

"Minimum illumination," said the First Officer, and Gil doused his light.

The only sounds between them was of worried breathing.

* * *

The Skiff…

Jai-Lan Wèi slowly maneuvered the skiff to the far side of the vessel, keeping a lookout for a hiding place. One by one, she shut down everything except her Nav panel and Conn, relying on her E-suit communicator for talking to the ship. Finally, she realized she couldn't see a thing outside without her skiff's exterior lamps. She hit the switch.

There.

A row of reflective panels hung below the underside of the vessel, and she deftly swung the skiff beneath them. She nudged the tiny lifeboat upward until it "clunked" gently against the vessel surface, activated the magnetic coupler on the top, and shut down all main power. She thought to contact *Pheidippides*, but knew Murphy would prefer radio silence. She sat back to wait, listening to the comm channel from the ship. She waited. Fifteen minutes went by uneventfully. Then twenty.

She rubbed her belly absently, thinking of Martin's words to her. *"I'm only twenty-six, and just not ready to settle down, you know?"*

She scowled to herself. *Yeah, Martin, I know. I'm only twenty-three, and this isn't what I planned either, but here we are.*

He'd stammered through a few clichés, offered a weak smile, and simply gotten up and left. No *"we'll work this out"*, no *"I'm willing to give it a try for the sake of the child"*, just… left. Walked out of her quarters and her life, as if he could do that on a ship like *Pheidippides*. Or anywhere.

Fine. I'll deal with it. You made your call. Goodbye.

She thought about Murphy's comment then, her *"believe me, I understand your situation"*.

Oh, God… what if she meant it literally?

* * *

EAS Pheidippides…

"One million kilometers, Captain!" Demarcy at Tactical nearly stood, then looked to Murphy.

"Take it easy, Lieutenant. Karen, what have you got?

"Pacing us, Captain, holding position, no hostile moves."

Murphy considered her options, which were few. *Pheidippides* had a grand total of four photon torpedoes, and particlebeams that were good for about two minutes without recharging. She knew they could outrun anything the Qoearc had, but she wasn't about to leave her boarding party. Besides that, there was little available but destroying the vessel to keep it from the Qoearc. She knew that was a court martial offense, but it all sort of fit her history.

Murphy waited thirty seconds before she spoke again. "Status?"

"No change, Captain," said Demarcy.

"Ditto, Captain," said Karen Connor at Nav.

Jules O'Brien looked over his shoulder from Conn, waiting for orders.

"Martin, open a channel, general hail." Murphy waited until he nodded to her. "Attention intruder. This is Lieutenant Commander Jenni Murphy of *EAS Pheidippides*. You have entered an interdict zone. The vessel nearby is property of the Earth Alliance and under the protection of Earthfleet. State your origin, authority, and purpose, or withdraw immediately from this area. Failure to comply may result in our use of deadly force."

"Wow." Demarcy mumbled under his breath, and Murphy shot him a withering glance.

"Captain, something is happening…" Connor shook her head as a ship materialized on the screen.

Murphy's jaw nearly dropped to the floor.

"Captain Jameis Adams, EAS Lawrence. Pleased to meet you, Commander." The image changed to an Earthfleet Bridge, and a bearded human male in the command chair, smiling into the pickup.

"Captain, that's a *Dolander*-class heavy transport," said Demarcy.

"It sure is," breathed Murphy, regaining her composure. She sat straighter in her seat. "Happy to see you, Captain. Very happy, actually." She paused. *What the hell?*

Murphy licked her lips before continuing. "Might I ask how you found us? This isn't exactly a well-traveled route."

"Orders, Commander," replied Adams. *"We received the same OC as you."*

Oh ho, I said, said I... Murphy grinned, knowing if she didn't, she would probably grimace at the transparency of what was happening. "And now, I assume you're here to haul this thing back to Fleet Base Twenty-three, right?"

Adams was noncommittal. *"We'll be taking charge of this operation. Your orders are to head to Fleet Base Twenty-three immediately."*

Murphy nodded to herself. "Permission to escort you back to base, Captain. There are still Qoearc afoot in the area."

"Lawrence is capable of handling any situation, Commander. Permission denied, but thank you."

"Even when you're towing half a million kilos of cargo? Sort of cuts down on your maneuverability, I'll bet."

Adams lost his ingratiating smile. *"As said, your orders are to return to base. No exceptions. Get moving, Commander."*

Looks passed around the Bridge as Murphy's jaw clenched. "I have a boarding party on the vessel I need to retrieve. Give us an hour and we'll get back to you." She made a throat-cutting gesture to Teng-Hey at Comm. The screen changed to the vessel and *Lawrence* now closing on it. "Go to Standby Alert. And get me the skiff, quick!"

Martin turned to his instruments, then back to Murphy. "She's on, Captain."

"Jai-Lan, we've got Earthfleet company."

"I heard, Captain. Orders?"

"Get the boarding party out as soon as possible, but don't rush. Safety first."

"Captain, they've gone to radio silence, and Lieutenant Ch'rehrin sent a quick fleettext just before, saying it would be thirty minutes before we heard from them."

Murphy glanced at the chronometer. "About ten minutes from now. That gives you time to get to the entry hatch. Be careful. Keep yourself as hidden as you can while you move. I don't trust this Captain Adams any farther than I can probably throw him." *Which I'd like to do right now. Damn regs, anyway.*

"Understood, Captain. Getting underway now."

Murphy clicked off. "Martin, did *Lawrence* call back?"

"No, Captain. Nothing."

Murphy nodded slowly. "Maybe we'll get out of this alive after all."

* * *

The Boarding Party…

It took all of the ten minutes and a bit more, for Jai-Lan to maneuver the skiff from hiding and around the curve of the vessel to the entry hatch. She waited as the ship slowly rotated, so the hatch would be beyond sight of *Lawrence* before the skiff drifted into place.

Ch'rehrin had called; the boarding party was outside and waiting. It took another fifteen minutes for everyone to cross and get into the airlock.

"Stay put," Jai-Lan radioed to the others, "I'm taking us back to *Pheidippides* as quickly as possible. We've got company."

Ch'rehrin, Gil, and Ball braced themselves in the airlock as they could, as Wèi swung the skiff around and headed for *Pheidippides*, a hundred kilometers distant. Another twenty minutes and they were docked. Ball and Gil exited quickly, but Ch'rehrin hung back and cornered Jai-Lan as she came into the airlock.

"Ensign, why did you take such chances with us in the airlock. You know the regulations."

"Captain's orders, sir. She said get back as quickly as possible."

"*Lawrence* is an Earthfleet vessel. Surely they are here to assist us."

Wèi nodded. "I fully agree, sir, but we're back safely, and I have duty on the Bridge. Please excuse me."

She passed by and into the docking bay. Ch'rehrin raised an eyebrow. "She seems to be acquiring some of the captain's mannerisms," he muttered to himself.

* * *

EAS Pheidippides…

"Contact *Lawrence*, get me Captain Adams, please." Murphy had taken time to compose her thoughts as the skiff docked. She watched the Bridge stations, all manned now by A-shift personnel and seconds standing by as necessary.

Jai-Lan Wèi stood uncomfortably at the Comm station as Martin Teng-Hey watched the instruments. At last, Murphy motioned her to the command seat. "Stay here with me, Ensign. Tell me what you see when we speak with *Lawrence*."

"Aye, Captain."

The screen lit. *"I trust your skiff is back aboard with all hands safe."* Adams's face was neutral, and his words were not a question, Murphy noted.

"Correct, sir. *Pheidippides* is preparing to get underway to Fleet Base Twenty-three now. Just making sure everything is secured in the docking bay."

"Excellent. Well done, Commander. Give my regards to the Admiral."

"Which admiral would that be, sir?"

Adams's face went rigid. *"The admiral in charge of Fleet Base Twenty-three, of course. I don't recall his name."*

"So… you aren't taking this vessel back to Fleet Base Twenty-three, Captain? Might I ask where it's going?"

"Not your concern, Commander. Get going. That's an order."

"Yes, sir. *Pheidippides* out." Murphy hit the switch. "Hatu, is that neutrino source you detected days ago still out there somewhere.?"

"Yes, Captain, still barley at detection range."

"And likely *Lawrence* doesn't know it." Murphy drew a breath. "Okay, here is where things get interesting." She punched the intercom switch again. "Engineering, Bridge. Taylor, what's our best speed, damn the safety factors."

A pause. *"Captain, we could hit 220c for about eight minutes if I turn off all the safeties. Other than that, 200c for several hours."*

"Thanks, Taylor. Stand by for max hyperlight." Murphy hit the switch again and looked to Wèi. "What's Adams hiding?"

Jai-Lan considered. "Pretty obvious, Captain. They're not going back to Fleet Base Twenty-three, and they're not telling us anything. He's anxious to get us out of the area."

"And he's made no move to take the vessel in tow." Murphy mused. "This stinks."

"Captain, *Lawrence* is maneuvering to attach its docking pad to the vessel," reported Gil.

"About time. Keep an eye on that neutrino source, Hatu. Karen, *Lawrence* is your job to follow, regardless where they or we go, as long as they're in range."

"Captain, what are your concerns?" Ch'rehrin looked from his panel to Murphy.

"Simple caution. There are Earth Alliance citizens on board the vessel, and it's in my oath to protect them."

All eyes went to Murphy.

"Not citizens as written in the law," replied Ch'rehrin, quietly.

"This isn't a matter of law, Mr. Ch'rehrin. My decision, my authority, my responsibility."

Ch'rehrin paused. "Very well, Captain." He turned back to his panel.

"Thank you, Captain," whispered Wèi. Murphy laid a hand across the Ensign's.

"Pheidippides, Lawrence. Why are you still here, Commander?" Adam's face showed again on the screen, obviously unhappy with Murphy's presence.

Murphy forced a smile. "Sorry, sir, none of us have ever seen a docking maneuver quite like this, and we were just curious. Thanks for the show. Nicely done."

Adams's posture relaxed slightly. *"Very well. Be on your way, and Godspeed, Pheidippides."* The screen darkened again.

"Tactical, give me a view of the area where the neutrino source is. Helm, ahead one-quarter sublight. Karen, watch *Lawrence*, tell me their heading once they're underway. Comm, we're going to prepare a squirt to Fleet Base Twenty-three in just a bit, if what I think is going to happen, happens. Make sure it's all recorded and in the log." Murphy turned to Wèi. "Back to your post, Ensign."

Jai-Lan smiled softly, stepped away, and Murphy faced the screen, watching with intent.

* * *

For long minutes after *Pheidippides* accelerated away, *Lawrence* remained, for all intents and purposes, motionless. Connor at Nav reported to Murphy, as Hatu Gil monitored the general area, focusing the best sensors and detection equipment in Earthfleet on the transport, the vessel now held in the docking cradle, and the border, nearly a light year distant. And the still-elusive neutrino source, seen, then not seen, but always on the fringes of detection.

"Still clear, Captain," reported Hatu from Tactical.

"Then why aren't they moving?" Murphy shook her head, eyes searching the screen for something, anything, to explain the odd behavior of *Lawrence* and its commanding officer.

"They're sending out a shuttle to the vessel," reported Connor at Nav. "I knew it."

Murphy nodded. "Keep an eye on them, Lieutenant, tell me of any change or if they try to board."

"Captain, I have a spike," said Ch'rehrin from the Science station. "Approaching *Lawrence* from galactic south, the border area, heavily stealthed and fast. No identification, but definitely a neutrino source."

"Confirmed." Gil glanced to Murphy, who nodded and showed a nearly-feral grin. She touched the intercom button. "Engineering, Bridge. Taylor, I want to fade us out very slowly into full stealth mode. Set it up and send the commands to Tactical. Very slowly, Chief."

"You want a 'fade to black', Captain?" Thomas chuckled on the intercom. *"Yeah, we can do that. Two minutes."*

"Mr. O'Brien, once we're stealthed, hard about one-eighty. Stand by for hyperlight. Karen, what's *Lawrence* up to?"

"Nothing yet, just sitting there. Wait… okay, they're moving now, about one-quarter sublight, heading… well, basically the way they were pointed." Connor turned slightly to face Murphy. "They have to be aware of the spike."

"What about the shuttle?"

Connor watched her instruments. "Turning about now, but… they'll never make it back to *Lawrence* in time."

"This Captain Adams is an idiot. They should be accelerating to engage hyperlight, but they're not, because they have to wait for the shuttle. They're just a target… aren't they, Mr. Gil?"

Gil shook his head. "Sure looks that way, Captain. Orders?"

"Once we're stealthed, go to Battle Stations, arm all weapons." Murphy hit the intercom again. "Sickbay, Bridge. Doc, you there?"

"Here, Captain. There is so much tension on this ship, I can feel it."

Murphy rolled her eyes. "You should be on the Bridge. I just want to let you know, we're heading into a combat situation. Prepare as necessary."

A pause. *"I see. Very well, we will make preparations as we may. Trust your feelings, Captain, and you will do as you must."* Melinkov clicked off.

"Bridge, Engineering, this is Thomas. We're ready to go, Captain. Commands sent to Tactical."

"Thanks, Taylor. Hang on back there, this could get bumpy." Click.

"Captain! Ship appearing now, fifty thousand kilometers off the stern of *Lawrence*!"

"Cripes, I knew it! Fade us out, Tactical! Battle Stations." Murphy waited as the Bridge lights dimmed to red. "Helm, come about, 80c now!"

Pheidippides leapt.

An explosion blossomed at the rear of the vessel towed by *Lawrence*. The transport stayed its course and did not return fire, waiting for the shuttle, still five minutes from the transport's hangar.

"Qoearc, Captain, heavy scout configuration. They have twice our firepower and their hull is dense." Ch'rehrin's voice was calm as he monitored his readings.

"Drop from hyperlight, stand by weapons." Murphy scooted to the edge of her command seat. "Comm, send this in clear, broad wave." Teng-Hey nodded after a moment. "Qoearc vessel, this is *EAS Pheidippides*. You are ordered to cease your attack on the *EAS Lawrence* and its cargo and immediately withdraw, or we will fire. You have ten seconds, mark."

"Qoearc firing again, Captain!"

"Still no return fire from *Lawrence*," reported Ch'rehrin.

"*Lawrence* course unchanged." Connor's eyes scanned her console. "Shuttle three minutes out."

"Damage to the vessel, nothing critical, central core is still intact," said Ch'rehrin calmly.

"Ten seconds, Captain." Ch'rehrin turned to Murphy as she nodded.

"Tactical… fire torpedo, full PAKS for thirty seconds. Hit them hard, Hatu, then reload, and hit them again."

Pheidippides's single torpedo tube glowed, and particlebeam emitters ran to the redline, then reset. The Qoearc ship shook from bow to stern, but fired a third time on the derelict vessel.

"*Lawrence* still not returning fire, still not changing course!"

"Easy, Connor, we got their attention, didn't we?"

"Damage to the vessel increasing, Captain, Two or three more hits will reach the core." Ch'rehrin glanced to Murphy. "We must draw them off."

Connor grimaced. "Qoearc vessel is swinging around, headed our way."

"Hatu, do we have PAKS back yet?"

"Thirty seconds, Captain."

"Helm, let's see if they want to play chicken. Straight at 'em."

O'Brien swallowed hard. "Straight at 'em, Captain."

"Go!"

Ten seconds, and the Qoearc vessel veered off. Murphy nearly shouted.

"PAKS online, Captain."

"Helm, get on their tail! Hatu, spank them hard!"

O'Brien swung *Pheidippides* around and pressed for acceleration. Gil hit his controls. The rear of the Qoearc ship exploded. Particlebeams raked the engines, and they exploded as well. Seconds later, the rest of the intruder followed, spreading debris in every direction.

"Back us off, Helm, get us out of that debris field!"

Pheidippides swung wide, hot junk from the Qoearc ship glancing off the hull.

"No breaches," reported Ch'rehrin. "Minor damage aft and near the main sensor, all instrumentation still functioning."

"Martin, you got all of that on full recordings, right?"

"Aye, Captain, every bit. Vid, comm, everything. Including *Lawrence* playing target. Backing up the files now." His face was nearly white.

"Get that off to Fleet Base Twenty-three immediately, full scramble, full encryption." Murphy paused. "And another copy to Earth Main, tagged to the Admiralty."

"Captain?" Martin looked askance at Murphy.

"That would be most unusual, Captain," said Ch'rehrin mildly, from his post. "But under the circumstances, prudent."

"Objections?"

Ch'rehrin was silent for a moment. Eyes around the Bridge crept his way. "Simply an observation."

Murphy nodded without smiling. "Good. Martin, get *Lawrence* please."

Teng-Hey worked his controls. "They're on, Captain."

The screen lit with the face of Captain Adams. *"Pheidippides, is your ship safe? And why are you back in this sector?"*

"We're fine. Just saving your ass. Sir."

"You were under a direct order to get underway, Commander."

Murphy scoffed under her breath. *That's what I thought.* "Captain, I must inform you, I've sent a full report to Fleet Base Twenty-three regarding this little encounter. Including identification of the Qoearc ship, their firing on an Earth relic, and your ship's reluctance to return fire to protect your cargo or *Lawrence,* not to mention the tactical error of sending an unarmed shuttle to your cargo while a known hostile was in the area."

A trickle of sweat made its way down Adams's temple. *"I don't know what you're talking about."*

"Of course you don't," said Gil quietly from his station. Murphy glanced his way.

"Where are you taking the vessel, Captain? We're all curious."

"That's classified, Commander. And when I reach my destination, Earthfleet will hear about this situation and your total insubordination."

"Yes, I'm sure they will. But they'll hear about your dereliction of duty first. Have a safe trip, Captain. *Pheidippides* out." Murphy hit the switch, sitting back.

"Orders, Captain?" Ch'rehrin stood by the command chair, his face showing only mild curiosity.

Murphy watched the image of *Lawrence* and its cargo for a quiet moment. "Tactical, stand down from Battle Stations, but keep your eyes open. Helm, ahead full sublight, course for home. Karen, watch *Lawrence* as long as you can. Let me know when they're out of range before we go to hyperlight. Martin, make sure your recorders are still on." She took a breath. "Once *Lawrence* is out of range, 220c to Fleet Base Twenty-three."

A chorus of "Aye, Captain" went around the Bridge. Murphy stood slowly. "Mr. Ch'rehrin, you have the conn. I think I'm gonna go throw up."

* * *

"Captain, this is Ch'rehrin. I have the report you requested."

Murphy rolled in her bunk and sat up, breathing heavily. The dreams had come again, and she was drenched in sweat. *I thought this would put an end to them, but I guess I was wrong.*

She pressed the intercom button. "Conference niche, fifteen minutes." She clicked off and buried her face in her hands, waiting for her heartbeat to calm. *I need a real shower and breakfast.*

She glanced at the chronometer; 1300 Hours. She'd been asleep since night watch ended, after spending most of it on the Bridge. She rose, stretched, and headed for the shower room, grabbing a clean jumpsuit as she exited.

Twenty minutes later, coffee and pastry in hand, she entered the conference niche where Ch'rehrin was waiting.

She sat. "Okay, what do we have?"

Ch'rehrin handed her his PADD. Murphy perused it, sipping. "No real damage, no casualties, we fired three torpedoes, and burned out a PAKS emitter. And full recordings of the event, right?"

"Yes, Captain."

After a bite and another sip of coffee, she asked, "How's the crew? Any concerns or questions?"

"Many, and I am certain a word from you would be helpful."

"They performed well, don't you think?"

"Certainly, Captain, considering the circumstances."

Murphy studied Ch'rehrin. "And you? You seemed to have concerns on the Bridge regarding my handling of the situation."

The first officer shook his head. "None serious, after what was seen by everyone."

Murphy set away the PADD. "Do you find it interesting neither Earthfleet ship was fired on by the Qoearc?"

Ch'rehrin considered for a moment. "But in a way, not surprising, assuming your theory of a planned ambush is correct. Should we have sustained combat damage, it would support our claim of attack. Obviously, the Qoearc knew of the derelict and used it as a lure."

"Thanks for not blurting that out on the Bridge, by the way." Murphy smiled over her coffee cup.

"I deduced it was your thought, and kept silent for obvious reasons."

Murphy drained her cup and set it down. "Why didn't *Lawrence* return fire? That's one question I still can't answer."

Ch'rehrin called up a graphic on the PADD and turned it to Murphy. "Lieutenant Gil analyzed the attack. The Qoearc scout approached from below and behind the derelict, effectively neutralizing *Lawrence's* field of fire. Further, had *Lawrence* maneuvered to bring their PAKS weapons to bear, it would have put the shuttle at risk."

Murphy nodded, eye to eye with her first officer. "What's your assessment of *Lawrence's* response to everything else?"

Ch'rehrin's face grew pensive. "I have considered that very subject and find no explanation for their behavior."

"I agree. How about a wild idea?"

"I am… at a loss, Captain."

She paused for effect. "Politics."

Ch'rehrin was silent, then nodded.

"What do you think will happen when we arrive at Fleet Base Twenty-three? In the end, I mean."

Ch'rehrin thought for a moment. "Certainly, there will be a board of inquiry in time. Assuming *Lawrence* is going to Earth Main Base, which is the reason you sent the information packet, it will take several months travel with the cargo in tow…" His voice trailed at her look.

"What proof do we have they're taking it anywhere? As I said, politics."

"I am not certain what you mean—"

"I don't know what I mean either, but when we arrive at Base, I expect to be arrested and thrown in the brig. After that…"

"Captain, you defended another Earthfleet ship and a relic of historic significance. While you technically disobeyed a direct order, had you followed it, we cannot postulate what might have happened."

Murphy shook her head. "I can."

"In a court of law, that would be supposition, and not admissible."

"Thanks, Ch'rehrin, you're really cheering me up."

"Captain, it would be against all reason for Earthfleet to charge you with anything beyond minor insubordination. Further, it may be argued the order you disobeyed was not a lawful order."

"So you're a lawyer now?"

Ch'rehrin straightened. "I hold two degrees in law, and I am licensed to practice on both Arnec and Earth."

Murphy's eyes widened. "I… had no idea. Okay, you're hired."

"Captain?"

"To be my defense attorney at trial. What's your retainer fee?"

* * *

"Two hours to Base, Captain. We've received docking orders and our approach vector."

"Thanks, Chuck. All-ship comm, please." Murphy waited as Honley attended his panel.

"You're on, Captain."

"Attention *Pheidippides* crew, this is Murphy. We're nearly home after eight months in deep space with only ourselves and each other for company. After what we've been through in the last few weeks, I'd say this ship deserves a vacation.

"It's my pleasure to inform you that I've requested and received approval for thirty day's leave for everyone once we reach Fleet Base Twenty-three. Also, for the hard work and dedication you've shown to Earthfleet and Alliance principles, an official Letter of Commendation will be placed in your files."

She paused for a breath. "On a more personal note, should this be our last mission together, I want to say how proud I am to have served with you as your commanding officer. Scout duty is tough, even for the best of us. *Pheidippides's* crew is top of the line. Whatever future duties we have, I wish you all the best. Murphy out." She clicked off and set back, letting go a breath.

"Excellent, Captain." Doctor Melinkov stood beside the command chair.

"Didn't hear you come in, Doc. You're not often on the Bridge."

"True, and I was in the laboratory when I heard your communique start. I decided it was time for a visit."

"Personal or professional?" Murphy turned to face her.

"Perhaps a bit of both." Melinkov looked at the main viewer. "It will be good to see the stars with our own eyes, not depicted in on a screen, yes? And to walk in the park with trees and greenery."

"Wasn't much of that on the planet we were dirtside on, was there?"

Melinkov was quiet for a moment. "I will tidy up Sickbay and the laboratory, Captain. Once we have docked and debarked, I should like to see you in my on-base office."

Murphy nodded slowly. "Sure. Just let me know when."

"Twenty-four hours after docking should be sufficient time for us to settle in, do you think?"

"I'll put it on my comm."

Melinkov turned and left. Murphy watched her disappear through the doors. *What the hell was that all about?*

"Captain." Ch'rehrin stepped from his Science station and approached. "I have researched the topic of our previous conversation." He lowered his voice and leaned toward Murphy. "Under your command, I cannot represent you legally. However, once released from this mission, it may be possible, should you still be… concerned."

Murphy smiled. "It's okay, Mr. Ch'rehrin. Whatever is going to happen will happen. But thank you. I'll keep it in mind."

Ch'rehrin nodded, and returned to his station.

"Coming up on the defense perimeter, Captain."

"Take us out of hyperlight, Helm. One quarter sublight."

O'Brien hit the controls. A shudder went through the ship. He looked nervously over his shoulder at Murphy. "Out of hyperlight, one quarter sublight, aye."

Murphy pressed the intercom switch. "Engineering, Bridge. Taylor, what was that?"

"Wear and tear on the phase coils, Captain. Pheidippides needs an overhaul. Maybe a full refit."

She let out a nervous breath. "Just get us home in one piece. Please."

"One piece, aye." Thomas chuckled before he broke the link.

Murphy's wrist comm beeped with an incoming fleettext.

REPORT TO THE COMMANDING ADMIRAL'S OFFICE ON ARRIVAL. NO DETOURS. BURKE.

Murphy sat back, exhaling in a huff. *Cripes, that tears it. And the Doc's little visit figures into this too, I'll bet.*

* * *

Commanding Admiral Tobias Burke was old enough to be Murphy's grandfather. In fact, he *was* her grandfather, on her maternal side. Tall and built like a barrel, with a crown of white hair and beard to match, he was as imposing as anyone Murphy had ever met. And she'd known him all her life.

She hadn't known he was the commandant of Fleet Base Twenty-three when *Pheidippides* was assigned to the sector, and had not seen her grandfather for two years before that. But on her first arrival, they'd shared dinner, and agreed to speak of it to no one else on the station or aboard her ship.

Therefore, Doc's little visit to the Bridge was to let me know she knew, and wanted to "chat" about it afterward.

Murphy's boots clicked on the immaculate hallway surface as she entered the Admiralty section. She stopped at the scanner, inserted her Earthfleet ID, put her finger in the DNA analyzer, and stared into the retinal scanner. Then stuck her tongue out at the screen as it displayed a cheery "Welcome to the Admiralty" message. The doors parted, and she entered.

She'd never been in an admiral's office before. There were two security guards at a far desk, two more aside, and a large screen on the wall opposite them. She knew behind the screen were likely more guards, and some pretty heavy stun equipment. Maybe even real weapons.

"ID, please". She handed her ID to the sergeant, who scanned it again, then offered a visitor's badge. "We'll hold this until you're done, Commander."

Murphy nodded.

The second guard rose. "This way, please."

The door into the office proper was built like the access to a safe. Murphy entered, and the door closed behind her.

Admiral Burke sat behind a desk not quite as large as *Pheidippides's* entire Bridge. He motioned to a chair before it, and Murphy sat.

"What's this, Commander?" Burke held a memory crystal in his hand.

Great. No "glad you made it back safely" no "well done", no "how's my favorite granddaughter", nothing. Murphy swallowed. "I have no idea, sir. I might guess it's the message *Pheidippides* sent after the… encounter with the derelict ship and *EAS Lawrence.*"

"Don't forget the Qoearc scout you destroyed."

"...I haven't, sir."

"Now, as I said, what is this?"

Murphy made a leap of faith. "The same question I've been asking. I had hoped to get some answers when we got back. That's why I sent the message, sir."

"And you sent a copy to Earth Main, correct?"

"Yes, sir."

"Why?"

"... Insurance."

Burke nodded, but didn't smile. "Very well. I can accept that. I won't accuse you of going over my head, under the circumstances."

"I had no intention of that, sir."

Burke shuffled papers, then held up a sheet. "Do you know what this is?"

"Sir, with all respect, can we just cut to the chase? I know I'm going to be hauled up on all sorts of charges, but I did what I thought was right. If you've reviewed my report, I'm sure you understand my concerns."

"Earthfleet is not in the business of concerns, Commander."

"Begging the admiral's pardon, sir, but we are. There are frozen embryos of Earth Alliance citizens in cryogenic deep-freeze on board that ship, citizens from hundreds of years ago. They have rights."

"Not as the Earth Alliance law is written currently, Commander."

Murphy fumed. "Screw the law! Those are people! Sir."

Burke studied her for a long moment. "Do you know anything about Captain Adams?"

Murphy blinked. "No, sir. Nothing other than what I gleaned from our conversations during the… event."

"He's a second cousin."

Murphy shook her head, not understanding.

"He's family."

Murphy opened her mouth to speak, then closed it. She had no words.

"I sent you and him out there because I needed people I could trust."

"… Sir?"

"To do the right thing."

Murphy held her breath for a long time. "May I ask, exactly what you mean? Sir?"

"You may ask," replied Burke, with a half-smile.

Murphy's hands were trembling, and she clutched them together tightly. "So… it's going to be alright?" She cast a surreptitious glance around the cavernous office, knowing every utterance and gesture was likely being recorded.

Burke nodded slightly. "You know there will be an official board of inquiry regarding everything that happened. But the situation can be reviewed, and sometimes laws from the past invoked. The term is "Grandfathering", if you're not familiar with it."

Burke chuckled, as Murphy sat wide-eyed and silent. "A little joke, but I see you're in no mood for it. Therefore, yes, Commander. To answer your question, everything is going to be alright. It will take time, but we're moving in the right direction."

He tossed the memory crystal to her. "Keep that. As a reminder of who you are." His voice dropped to nearly a whisper. "Your mother would have been proud." He stood, as did Murphy. "Dismissed, Commander."

She left the Admiralty in a daze, tears of joy stinging in her eyes.

* * *

Murphy had wandered the Base gardens for hours when Doctor Melinkov approached from a side path.

"Good morning, Commander. You are up very early."

Murphy nodded listlessly. "Not much sleep last night. None, in fact. I've been up since we got in yesterday."

"Perhaps we may have tea." Melinkov motioned to a small tea house off the flowered walkway.

They sat and were served. Murphy drank quietly, lost in thought.

"You have worries again, yes?"

Murphy shrugged. "Actually, no, Doc. For the first time in a while, I don't think I do."

"What has brought this change of heart, if I may ask?"

"I really don't..." Murphy paused. "Let's just say a guardian angel might have given me a break."

Melinkov sipped tea before speaking. "Excellent. If this is truly the case, you will give thanks in time, I'm certain. And now?"

"We have thirty days leave. After that, I'm not sure. I haven't checked the mail." She tapped her wrist comm. "No beeps, so I don't have new orders yet."

"What would be your desire, if I may ask?"

Murphy shrugged again. "Doc, you're laying it on too thick. I'm exhausted, spent, and right now, all I want to do is find a bed."

Melinkov nodded. "In that case, I do have a bit of news for you that should lift your spirits. Martin and Jia-Lan are talking."

Murphy's face brightened. "That's great. I hope they can work it out. They're great kids."

The doctor smiled. "Not so much younger than yourself, Commander, to call them children."

They laughed together.

"I will postpone our office visit until tomorrow, Commander. But I expect to see you then. I will send the time to your comm." Melinkov rose. "Good day, and have a pleasant rest."

"Thanks, Doc. See you tomorrow."

Murphy watched as Melinkov walked away, her mind adrift. *He trusted me to do the right thing, because I know his thinking on the subject. And Mom's. I know the choice she made, and the one I made, too. And I damn near messed it all up anyway. So close…*

She rose at last, headed back to Officer Country, and a room that wasn't the same she'd slept in for eight months straight.

After years of living with the fear of a wrong decision once again, and trepidation running rampant through her soul, she knew it really was going to be alright.

Just like Grandad said.

About the Author

Dennis Young's writing experience began somewhere around the third grade and has continued since. Once through the grueling trials of school (grade, high, and college level, surviving all with a flourish) he found an outlet for his imagination in the world of fanzines and fan literature. Writing for friends, family, and once in a while actual publication, his appetite was only whetted.

Working in the International Construction industry, he found opportunity to direct his writing talents to presentations, articles, and project management.

In the early 2000's he began assembling The Ardwellian Chronicles, an Epic Fantasy Saga of six novels and three compendiums totaling more than 1.3 million words.

With the Chronicles published between 2007 and 2018, he then turned to the genre of Military Science Fiction and The Mercenary Trilogy, detailing the adventures of Talice Wyloh.

His next foray was into SF adventure and The Earthfleet Saga Volumes One and Two, with further books in the works.

Never one to say no to a challenge, more genres lay in the future for his exploration.

Stay tuned…

Website – Ardwel.com
Website – dennisyoung64063.wixsite.com/author-dennis-young
Facebook – Working on the Ardwellian Chronicles and Hope I Live Long Enough to Finish
Facebook – Author Dennis Young
Blog – theardwellianchronicles.blogspot.com

Made in the USA
Middletown, DE
09 March 2019